DEAD IN THE WATER

In 1991 Dana Stabenow, born in Alaska and raised on a 75-foot fishing trawler, was offered a three-book deal for the first of her Kate Shugak mysteries. In 1992, the first in the series, *A Cold Day for Murder*, received an Edgar Award from the Crime Writers of America.

DANA STABENOW

"Kate Shugak is the answer if you are looking for something unique in the crowded field of crime fiction."
Michael Connelly

'For those who like series, mysteries, rich, idiosyncratic settings, engaging characters, strong women and hot sex on occasion, let me recommend Dana Stabenow.'
Diana Gabaldon

"A darkly compelling view of life in the Alaskan bush, well laced with lots of gallows humor. Her characters are very believable, the story lines are always suspenseful, and every now and then she lets a truly vile villain be eaten by a grizzly. Who could ask for more?" **Sharon Penman**

"One of the strongest voices in crime fiction." *Seattle Times*

"Cleverly conceived and crisply written thrillers that provide a provocative glimpse of life as it is lived, and justice as it is served, on America's last frontier." *San Diego Union-Tribune*

THE KATE SHUGAK SERIES

DANA STABENOW

DEAD IN THE WATER

HEAD
of ZEUS

First published in the UK in 2013 by Head of Zeus Ltd

Copyright © Dana Stabenow, 1993

The moral right of Dana Stabenow to be identified as the author
of this work has been asserted in accordance with the
Copyright, Designs and Patents Act of 1988.

9 7 5 4 6 8

A CIP catalogue record for this book is available from
the British Library.

ISBN (Paperback) 9781908800411

Printed and bound by CPI Group (UK) Ltd,
Croydon, CR0 4YY

Head of Zeus Ltd
Clerkenwell House
45-47 Clerkenwell Green
London EC1R 0HT

www.headofzeus.com

for Kathleen, Susan and Amy
co-writers in residence

and for Nancy, the angel at the gate

CHAPTER 1

THE *AVILDA* ROLLED INTO a trench of opaque green seas. Normally, when she was vertical, those seas rose as high as her masthead. Now the crabber was listing so steeply that the portside railing was awash. Kate, legs braced against the slant of the deck, had her head and shoulders jammed up against the frame of an empty crab pot. The pot was threatening to slide over her and the port rail in that order. Her arms were widespread; her fingers, numbed with cold and wet with salt water, clutched desperately to the frame of the pot. The wire mesh pressed into the flesh of her face. Something warm and liquid slid down her cheek. She wondered, without interest, if it was tears or blood.

The pot was seven feet tall and seven feet wide and three feet deep, a steel frame covered in metal netting, 750 pounds of dead weight empty. Kate was five feet tall, weighed just over 120 pounds and was mere flesh and bone, but she had Newton on her side, and she waited. She could feel the rest of the crew watching, but she was fiercely determined to do this herself, without help and, more importantly, without asking for help.

A muscle in her back rebelled at the unaccustomed strain and spasmed. She cursed beneath her breath, though if she'd

1

shouted her voice would not have been heard above the crash of Aleutian water on deck, the howl of Aleutian winds overhead and the rough, deep-throated roar of the engine beating up through the soles of her feet.

At last, at last, the crabber mounted the next swell and began its inevitable slide in the opposite direction. Groaning in every sheet of plate steel, her submerged hull began to roll and in one smooth, inexorable shift swung through the perpendicular. The killing pressure of the pot on Kate's shoulders eased. "For every action," she muttered as her feet pushed against the slippery deck, "there is an equal and opposite reaction. For every action, there is—"

The *Avilda* began her heel to starboard. With an involuntary sound, half grunt, half howl, in harmony with the shriek of the straining ship, Kate shoved with all her strength. The pot shuddered, moved a fraction of an inch, another, gave a sudden, stuttering lurch and began to slide. Kate, almost running to keep pace, shoved and slid and cursed her way behind it and across the deck, to fetch up against the opposite railing with a solid thump.

Behind her she heard Andy Pence give a whoop and a shout of approval mixed with amazement, and she thought she heard Seth Skinner swear in a tone distinctly admiring, but she was busy catching her breath. Besides, it was a point of honor not to acknowledge that she had done anything out of the ordinary. Panting, she clutched at the pot for support, fighting a wave of dizziness that made her close her eyes and lean her forehead against the cold, wet mesh. She tried to remember the last time she'd eaten something, anything. When she couldn't, she straightened painfully and looked around for the burly figure of the deck boss. "Hey! Ned!"

Ned Nordhoff looked as if he were wading through a nest

of pale spiders, up to his knees in the long, knobbled legs of tanner crab scrabbling frantically for purchase whether they were on their way into the hold as keepers or over the side and back into the Bering Sea. At Kate's shout, he looked up. She held up a hand, rubber-gloved fingers splayed, and jerked a thumb aft toward the cabin. He scowled, his hands barely checking. "You just went!"

Kate was soaked through to the skin and chilled through to the bone. Hunger had been gnawing on her for so long that her stomach fell like it was about to crawl up her esophagus. Her first, knee-jerk response to the deck boss's terse comment was anatomically impossible, her second sociologically taboo, both eminently satisfactory. She opened her mouth and a sheet of spray slapped her in the face, no bigger or harder than any such over the last week, but enough to ring two faces up before her eyes, side by side, wearing identical accusatory expressions, a macabre jackpot in a hellish casino.

Christopher Alcala.

And Stuart Brown.

That's all. Just two faces staring out at her from Jack Morgan's bulging file folder. Christopher Alcala, a thin, pale ascetic's face with big brown bedroom eyes, dark hair falling into them. He reminded Kate of her cousin Martin, when Martin was sober. And Stuart Brown, all fair curls and laughing eyes and wide grin. He looked cuddly, like an overstuffed teddy bear, and almost that mature.

Both Alcala and Brown had disappeared off the deck of the very ship upon which she was currently standing, more or less, not six months before, during the last fishing season. She was working Brown's spot.

Both of them very probably dead.

Both of them just twenty-one years old.

Kate looked at the mocking expression of the deck boss, who had been on board when Alcala and Brown disappeared and who may or may not have assisted in said disappearance, and let the furious words back up in her throat until she thought she might strangle on them. But it wasn't her job to tell the deck boss where he could get off, preferably into five hundred fathoms of North Pacific Ocean five hundred miles from Dutch Harbor, although, if God was good, that would come with time.

No, she was casual labor for the Anchorage District Attorney, for a price, and it was her job to find out what had happened to those two very young men. And Jack Morgan, one-time boss, part-time lover and full-time chief investigator for the Anchorage District Attorney, was paying her five hundred dollars a day, a hundred over his usual fee, to let the deck boss of this happy ship dump on her, if such was his pleasure. A hundred dollars extra was what it took to get her back on the deck of a boat again, and she knew a moment of bitter regret that it hadn't taken more. A lot more.

She took a deep breath, inhaling a little spindrift along the way, and sneezed. It knocked her off balance and she slipped on a deck that rejoiced in maintaining a surface halfway between ice and slime. "Shit!" she yelled, and caught at the railing on her way down. Her hip hit hard, the rubberized plastic of her rain gear caught and almost tore. She was back on her feet in an instant.

An unfriendly grin split the bearded face of the deck boss. Kate flipped him off, and he gave a short bark of laughter. "I'm going to grab something to eat!" she yelled over the sound of the waves.

He shrugged and gave a grudging nod. She groped hand over hand across the tilting deck to the galley's starboard door and fought her way inside. The boat heeled over into the down side of a swell and Kate waited, bracing herself against the bulkhead, until the *Avilda* righted herself and began a swing in the opposite direction. Using the listing motion as impetus she staggered across the galley floor, barely catching the handle of a cupboard with one wildly flailing hand. Drawing herself upright, she reached in and pulled out a box of Cheerios. Great. Oat bran. Just what she needed, food the manufacturer swore wouldn't give her cancer, might even in fact cure it. At the moment developing a nice little inoffensive cancer somewhere on dry land seemed infinitely preferable to what she was grimly convinced was soon to be her death by drowning way too far out at sea.

But they were the first edible thing that came to hand, they were calories, so far as she knew there were no moose steaks on board, and in the prevailing seas she wouldn't have been able to keep a frying pan on the stove long enough to cook them anyway. Bracing herself against the continuing pitch and roll of the deck beneath her, she raised the box, tilted her head back and caught a stream of cereal in her mouth. She chewed and swallowed and repeated the process. Tossing the box back into the cupboard and latching the door, she waited for the roll of the ship to be with her and staggered two steps to the refrigerator, from which she pulled a gallon of milk and drank a quart from the spout without drawing breath. Another step to the sink and four mugs of water followed the milk down.

As she was lowering the mug for the last time, she caught sight of the calendar swinging merrily back and forth on the opposite wall. It was October 21. Or was it October 22? She couldn't remember. They'd left Dutch Harbor the Tuesday before, she thought maybe October 15, but it was hard thinking that far back. Visions of the bunk just down the companionway danced like sugarplums in her head, her sleeping bag open and its red plaid flannel lining rough-smooth on her check. The illusion was so real that she took an involuntary step in its direction. Angrily, she gave herself a rough shake, all over, like a dog shaking water from its fur. Without sleep for so long, now she was hallucinating about it.

They'd been hot, "on the crab" for the last three days. The pots they'd set during their last run were coming up plugged with keepers and almost no garbage. They'd been humping it for thirty hours without so much as a sit-down dinner or a nap during that time. Or was it forty hours? She couldn't remember. Kate gave it up and pulled her way to and through the galley's portside door and around the cabin and back to the pot launcher.

Greeted by a slap of wind-driven salt spray, she wondered, with a spurt of irritation that surprised her because she didn't think she had the energy for anything except filling the next bait jar that came to hand, why the skipper persisted in powering through the troughs sideways, instead of bringing the ship around and catching them bow on. A flash of yellow caught her eye and she looked up to see Seth Skinner leaning over the rail to catch the next triad of buoys with a boat hook, a long pole with a sharp, curved hook on one end. He hauled in the sopping line hand over hand and when he had enough caught a length of it in the block. Line whipped through the winch, piling up on deck. Minutes later the pot's bridle broke the surface, followed immediately afterward by the pot. It was full of crab, loaded with crab, brimming with crab, overflowing with crab, and Kate didn't know whether to laugh or cry.

Seth Skinner, lean, lanky and imperturbable and who looked like Jimmy Stewart without the horse, pulled the ties that opened the pot door and the crab cascaded down to the deck. For a moment Kate stood still, looking at him speculatively. Seth Skinner, too, had been on board the *Avilda* the night Alcala and Brown had disappeared.

He raised his head suddenly and caught her looking at him. She met his gaze and held it, more curious than embarrassed. Seth's eyes were a clear gray and vacant of an identifiable expression, oddly peaceful. He smiled at her, a small smile that didn't touch his eyes and barely dented the corners of his mouth, and pulled on the pot, swinging it to one side.

"Shugak!" The shout was snatched out of the mouth of the deck boss and blew past her. She looked around. "You're on sorting!"

She nodded to show she understood. Waiting for the next swell, she caught the roll of the deck and slid to a position between pot launcher and hold, up to her knees in every kind of crab known to populate the bottom of the Bering Sea. Bending over, she began to sort through them mechanically. There were a few Dungeness, a couple of blue kings and one small and indignant squid, but mostly the pot was filled with tanners, *Chionoecetes bairdi* and *Chionoecetes opilio*. They were both thin, pale crab, with a light brown carapace and a yellowish under-shell, their legs long, slender and slightly flattened. The differences between them were slight. The *bairdi* weighed about a pound more. The *opilio* had smoother shells, slightly longer than they were wide, but otherwise to the untrained eye looked much the same as the *bairdi*. Kate decided it was like telling the difference between red and silver salmon; you had to get up close and personal to tell them apart. But not too close; she jerked back out of the reach of one snapping pincer just in time.

The season on *opilio* didn't open for another two months so they went back in the water. The *bairdi* were sorted for sex and size. A week's practice had made the six inchers easier to spot; the ones closer to the legal limit she checked with a curved piece of wood carved to fit over the crab's upper shell, measuring five and a half inches end to end. Males under five and a half inches and females were thrown back into the sea, the remainder into the hold, the trip into Dutch and a steam cooker all that remained of their immediate future.

Kate remembered reading somewhere that tanner crab could live up to fourteen years. It took six years for the female to mature and bear eggs. When she did, she could carry as many as 300,000 eggs. As tired as Kate was, she marveled every time she saw a bulging abdominal flap, and there was a certain reverence in the way she handled them. The males she tossed carelessly into the hold with the thousands of tanners already sloshing back and forth in the sea water that would keep them alive until they reached shore and the processor. Plenty more where they came from, or she wouldn't be standing up to her ass in them right now.

Bending once again to her task, she was somewhat shielded from the gusts of wind by the pot launcher and the railing, but the constant rocking back and forth made her head swim and her stomach churn. She knew better than to complain, though, and kept sorting.

About a year later the deck boss signaled the third deckhand to spell her, and she pulled her weary way over to the hold with arms that trembled in protest. She sat a moment on the edge, her numb hands beating some kind of response into the legs dangling into the hold, uncaring of the spray scouring the deck with a frozen hand.

"Get a move on those bait jars, Shugak!" Nordhoff barked.

A sudden rage, welcome because it warmed her, drove her to her feet and to the bait table butted up against the fo'c'sle. At that same moment a malicious gust of wind swirled around the boat and momentarily enveloped the foredeck in a miasma of diesel exhaust. The rage was as instantly replaced by nausea. She barely made it to the rail in time. Cereal, milk and water, all of it came up and then some, in retching, wrenching bursts that left her exhausted and trembling. Someone laughed, and it wasn't a nice laugh. It had to be Nordhoff. She hung, head down, wanting nothing so much as for the next wave to sweep her over the side and into the oblivion of a cold, wet and final embrace, anything to stop the heaving motion of her entire world.

All too soon, a voice boomed out. "Goddammit, get busy, Shugak!"

This time it was the captain's voice, bellowing down at her from an open window on the bridge, and this time when she struggled to repress her initial reply she saw Jack's face. Jack's entire body in a cast. Jack's tombstone, sans the Rest in Peace. She didn't want Jack to rest in peace. She wanted Jack to burn in hell.

Unable to summon up even enough energy to swear aloud, she called on every shaking muscle and pulled her way back to the bait table. The block of frozen herring was sliding back and forth with the heaving action of the *Avilda*, and she grabbed for it with one hand and for the big knife with the plastic handle with her other. On the first blow she brought the knife down too close to the fingers of the hand that held the herring.

She caught herself. The deck boss might be an asshole, the captain marginally competent and the rest of the crew either untrustworthy or unknown, but that didn't mean she had to behave recklessly herself. In fact, considering her reasons for being on board, it was imperative that she did not. She got a better grip on her temper and the knife and began to chop again, this time with more care.

The chunks of herring went into perforated plastic jars. Andy Pence, hired on the day after she was and who had learned everything he ever knew about crab fishing during the last six days, seven hours and thirty-six minutes of his life, staggered across the deck and gathered up an armful of the jars and went staggering back toward the empty pots lined up against the railing. One at a time, he plunged head and shoulders into the pots, hanging the bait jars inside and tying the doors shut on each afterward with lengths of yellow plastic twine.

Kate filled the last bait jar, tightened the lid down and waited for the deck beneath her feet to heave in the right direction. It did, but this time the swell was too big and she slid right past the stacked pots and into the pot launcher. It caught her just beneath her breasts, square across the diaphragm, knocking the breath out of her. Kate caught her breath just in time to hold it beneath the wave of spray that swept over the rail and poured ice-cold water inside her collar and down her spine. Gasping, she shook her head. When her eyes cleared she saw Seth Skinner grinning at her, his teeth a white slash in his bearded face. "Nice day!" he shouted. It was the longest sentence she'd ever heard him speak.

"Couldn't ask for nicer!" she shouted back, and fought her way over to where Andy was baiting. Together they baited the last pot, and Kate began coiling the twenty-five-fathom shots of five-eighth-inch polypropylene line while Andy checked the buoys. Each pot had three, one Styrofoam buoy and two air-filled plastic buoys, all painted a painfully fluorescent orange and each with the boat's name and registration number lettered on it in sloppy but legible black paint. Finishing with the buoys, he set his shoulder to the pot at the end of the row and reached around for the line fastening the pot down.

"No," Kate shouted, "wait for the next swell."

"What?" His usually fresh face was exhausted and uncomprehending.

He bent to shove and she grabbed his arm. "No," she shouted again, "wait. Wait."

The word penetrated, and dumbly, he waited.

The next swell was a big one, the biggest one yet. When she'd rolled as far as she was going to, the *Avilda's* portside gunnel was again awash, the water boiling over the railing. She hesitated there for a long, long moment. Kate knew enough of the old girl's construction to know that they'd loaded enough crab so that the *Avilda* was carrying sufficient ballast. Kate hoped. Just the same, she strained against the list of the deck, as if by pulling hard enough against the pot she could right the boat by her efforts alone. It was entirely involuntary, a human rebellion against this unnatural tilting of the world, and if she'd been able to look around she would have seen the rest of the crew, their faces screwed into similar fearful grimaces, straining just as hard against the nearest available surface.

The *Avilda* hesitated a moment longer, and then the swell passed beneath her keel and she heeled over with a rush. "Now!" Kate shouted. "Shove! Hard!"

Together, she and Andy shoved, hard, and the pot screeched across the deck, to be caught by Seth, who in a few deft movements had it attached to the hoist. He raised it to the pot launcher, Kate fastened off the shots of line and Andy lined up the buoys. Ned craned his neck and caught the nod from the bridge, and shifted the lever that tilted the pot launcher so that the pot slid over the side to crash into the heaving sea and begin its rapid journey to the muddy ocean floor some three hundred feet below. Kate heaved the coil of line after it, Andy the buoys. The process was repeated with the remaining five pots. After thirty—or was it forty?—straight hours of practice, the crew was moving well together, more of a team now, working about eight pots per hour. In good weather the really good boat crews worked between fourteen and eighteen pots per hour, but she didn't think this was one of them, and it sure as hell wasn't good weather, so they had done pretty well. She was almost proud of their performance. Just not enough to make a vocation out of it. She stretched, barely repressing a groan. Her body felt like a hockey puck after a sudden death play-off.

The skipper, a short, broad man with a short, broad face drawn into a perpetual scowl, appeared on the catwalk outside the bridge. He shouted and the deck boss looked up. The skipper made a circling motion with one forefinger.

The deck boss stuck up his thumb in reply and went aft, where he tossed out a short line with nothing on the end of it, letting it dangle down the side of the boat and trail in their wake.

It was the signal they had all been waiting for. On the bridge the skipper took a couple of turns on the wheel, and plunging and rolling as she came crossways of the heavy swell, the *Avilda* began to come about. Kate began gathering and coiling lines as the others stored the rest of the bait, secured the pots that needed mending, and replaced the hatch cover.

Dinner that night was whatever came to hand first. Kate, choking a little on the last bite of her peanut butter and grape jelly sandwich, stumbled through the door of her stateroom, feeling her way, eyes already closed in anticipation of hitting her bunk. Her foot tangled in something and she tripped and nearly fell. "What the hell?" Her bloodshot gaze peered around malevolently and encountered something that looked like a tent made out of a bedsheet, draped over three lengths of welding rod tied together in a kind of teepee frame.

Andy's sun-streaked mop of blond hair poked out of a fold of cloth. "It's okay, Kate, it's only me."

She stood where she was, swaying. "What the hell are you doing pitching a tent in the middle of the goddam floor? What's wrong with your bunk?"

He crawled out on all fours and rose to his feet. "It's not a tent, it's a pyramid."

"It's a what?" she said stupidly.

"A pyramid," he repeated. "I was reinforcing my *prana*."

"Reinforcing your *what*?"

"Reinforcing my *prana*." Andy picked up the top of the tent and it collapsed into a limp cylinder of linen and rods. "It's got the same ratio of structure as the pyramid at Giza."

Kate was very, very tired, or she never would have asked. "What's *prana*?"

He set the pyramid in a corner and looked at her, very solemn, very earnest. "*Prana* is the universal life force. All energy derives from it. It brings together East and West, the spiritual and physical. The pyramid concentrates that energy, and I meditate beneath it, thus enhancing my own personal *prana*." He stretched and yawned. "Long shift. Think I'll turn in." He climbed into the top bunk and burrowed beneath the covers. "Get the light, would you?"

CHAPTER 2

THE SMELL OF BACON frying brought Kate wide awake the next morning. For a moment she lay listening to the throb of the engines and the rush of the *Avilda*'s hull through the water. It wasn't necessary to hang on to anything to stay in her bunk. Of course. Now that they were no longer picking pots and hanging their asses out over the water, the high seas had abated. Naturally. Raising up on one elbow, she peered out the porthole.

All there was to see was fog and gray seas slipping rapidly past beneath it. It figured. This was the Aleutians. If it wasn't foggy, it was windy. If it wasn't windy, it was foggy. After the last week, Kate would take a nice, peaceful, impenetrable fog any day.

The tantalizing smell of bacon eventually proved impossible to resist. Abandoning the contemplation of things meteorological for things hygienic and things culinary, she showered and dressed, tied her still-wet hair back into a single braid and beat feet down to the galley. There she was greeted by the dizzying sight of eggs over easy, bacon fried crisp and a huge mound of buttered toast. It was the first hot meal she'd seen in four days. She piled her plate high and sat down next to Andy.

"Oh, no," he said, looking at her plate, "not you, too."

She reached for a slice of bacon. "I beg your pardon?"

He waited until the bacon was well and truly in her mouth.

"Oink, oink, oink, oink."

"Excuse me?"

"Meat eater," he said, in the portentous tone of one crying *"J'accuse!"*

She looked down at her plate, and was aware, not necessarily of things coming to a halt around her, but of attention being shifted to the two of them in an almost palpable way. "And proud of it," she agreed cheerfully, and forked up some egg.

"How can you be? Animals have souls," Andy told her, as earnest and as solemn as he had been the night before holding forth on *prana*, "the same as humans. Did you know that after death an animal may be reincarnated as a human, and vice versa?"

"Yes," Kate said calmly, taking the wind out of his sails and causing the other two men in the galley to look askance at each other and warily at her. Aleuts believed all things, animate and inanimate, had souls. She had learned that at her grandmother's knee, almost before she learned to walk, but she saw no reason to explain this to Andy.

"Well, then," Andy said, recovering, "don't you agree that it's wrong to kill animals unnecessarily? It interrupts their spiritual journey. It forces them to suffer another rebirth." Kate bit into a second slice of bacon and Andy, his voice rising slightly, said, "It upsets the cosmic scheme of things!"

Kate swallowed and said, "Define 'unnecessarily.'"

"What?"

"Define 'unnecessarily.'" Nonplussed, he didn't reply, and Kate said, "It's necessary for me to eat."

"But not meat," he said quickly.

"No?"

Her tone was mild. Andy sensed a potential convert. "You

can get everything you need, every essential vitamin, every mineral, all the nourishment your body requires for health and a long life from a vegetarian diet." Kate chewed bacon. "And without the senseless and wasteful slaughter of other living creatures!" Andy looked at her, his face expectant. If he'd had a tail, it would have been wagging.

Kate regarded him for a moment without expression, and returned to her bacon. He sighed, a gusty sigh of disappointment. He oinked once more but his heart wasn't in it. She ignored him, eating her way placidly through the rest of her bacon and eggs, watching him from the corner of her eye as she did so.

A little over two years back, in another life, when she had worked full-time instead of part-time for Jack Morgan, Kate's throat had been cut almost literally from ear to ear in an altercation with a gentleman caught in the act of abusing his four-year-old daughter at knifepoint. The gentleman was now deceased, and Kate's voice was now as scarred as her throat, a low husk of sound ranging anywhere from rough to rasping, and, when she chose, from harsh to horrifying. This morning she chose. Andy's mouth had barely closed on a heaping spoonful of granola when her scream ripped across the peaceful breakfast scene with all the soothing quality of a grizzly's claws ripping through flesh.

The eggs Ned was in the process of flipping had the frying pan jerked out from beneath them and they splattered across the stove top, and the rest of Harry's coffee splashed across the front of his shirt.

"Jesus! What the fuck is wrong with you?" Harry roared at her. Ned was cursing slowly and steadily over the charring mess on the stove. "What's going on?" Seth called down from the bridge.

She ignored them, watching Andy mop milk and cereal out of his lap with a shaking hand. He looked up and she caught his eye. She leaned forward and said in an oh-so-gentle voice, "Were you aware that scientists have recorded the screams of plants as they are picked?"

Andy's jaw dropped. He stared at her, speechless. In the ensuing silence, Ned turned away to hide a grin. A deep, rusty chuckle rumbled up out of Harry's chest.

Andy bent back over his cereal bowl without another word, and Kate bit into her last piece of bacon with relish.

● ● ●

After breakfast it was Kate's watch and she went up to the bridge to relieve Seth, who gave her a quizzical look, or as near to it as those bland gray eyes could produce. She responded with an equally bland smile.

Not five minutes after her butt hit the seat of the long-legged chair bolted to the deck next to the steering wheel, Harry Gault appeared on the bridge. He came to a stop next to her and waited, obviously expecting her to move so he could sit down.

She didn't budge. "Harry," she said calmly, "it's my watch, and I'm standing it. If you didn't trust me to steer this bucket, you should never have hired me on."

His answer was almost a snarl. "Like I had a say."

That was true enough, but Kate forbore to belabor the point. The fog was lifting a little, far enough to see a flat sea the same color as the fog rolling out in every direction. The automatic pilot was on, and all Kate had to do was mind the compass and watch for deadheads.

Harry stood there for another minute, his glower gathering

in force and ferocity. Kate glanced over at the radar, found a clear screen and began to hum a little beneath her breath. After a moment or two and another near snarl, Harry stamped back down the stairs into the galley. The slam of his stateroom door reverberated all the way up to the bridge, and Kate broke into song.

"'Tis a damn tough life full of toil and strife we whalemen undergo.'" She leaned forward to get a better look at a spot on the endless plain of water that turned out to be an Arctic tern, starting his 22,000-mile trip south a little late in her opinion. She sat back, hooked her toes over the top rung and thought about her skipper.

"'And we don't give a damn when the gale is done how hard the winds did blow.'" And then there were three, and the third was Harry Gault, skipper of the good ship *Avilda*, now and six months ago, when Alcala and Brown had disappeared. He was short, bulky and obstreperous, one of those men who took his lack of height out on every moving target that came within range. That and the fact that his seamanship was borderline competent were the only two things she knew about him. So far. Finding out more was why she was on board.

"'Now we're homeward bound 'tis a grand old sound on a good ship taut and free, and we won't give a damn when we drink our rum with the girls of old Maui.'" There was a tentative noise at the top of the stairs and she turned to see Andy Pence standing there, his expression indicating he had yet to forgive her for the scene at the breakfast table. "Hey there."

He directed his gaze at a point two inches above her left shoulder. "I was just on my way into the chart room."

She waved a benevolent hand. "Be my guest."

Fourth on the crew roster was Andy Pence, fresh off the beach of Ventura, California, seeking true adventure in the Far North, high as a kite on anything and everything Alaskan, and Kate's bunkie. Thus far, she had discovered that he meditated beneath a percale pyramid and didn't eat red meat. Last and most important, Andy Pence had been hired on after Kate, when the deckhand who had replaced Alcala had quit, and probably had nothing whatever to do with Alcala's and Brown's disappearance. At best, he was harmless; at worst, a hindrance. She thought back to the galley and grinned to herself. He was also, she hoped, a fast learner.

The rustle of stiff paper came from behind her. Curious, she checked the horizon and the autopilot and went back to see what Andy was up to.

The chart room stood aft of the wheelhouse. Andy was leaning his elbows on the tilted surface of the chart table, mooning over a marine chart. Kate stood up on tiptoe to peer over his shoulder. "What're you looking at the Shumagins for? That's a tad north of our heading, isn't it?"

Still very much on his dignity, he did not deem the question worthy of a civil reply. She smiled a little behind his back. He was so very young. The smile faded. As young as Stu Brown and Chris Alcala. She returned to the wheelhouse and hoisted herself back into the captain's chair, resuming her scan of the horizon. It was almost noon, and the fog was beginning to burn off.

It was one of those still winter days when the Cradle of the Winds lay calm and deceptively quiescent, gray sky and silver sea melding into a luminescent horizon without color or definition, a day handmade for dreaming. Old Sam Dementieff had shown Kate a picture of a very old map once, drawn when people thought the world was flat and square. On each edge the mapmaker had written "Beware—Heare Bee Dragons and Diverse Monsteres of Ye Deepe." It was that kind of day, a gift of a day, a day with dragons just over the next swell, a day when she didn't wince away from the thought of her father, or worry at the task that lay before her. The sea and the sky and the throb of the engine was all there was, and she settled back and gave herself up to it.

The knots rolled by. She heard the sounds of a chart being rolled and stowed. A moment later Andy appeared, still very much on his dignity. "Have some coffee," Kate said amiably, pouring him a mug from the thermos she'd brought topside with her.

"I'm not thirsty," he said stiffly.

"Have some anyway."

He took the mug because she might have dropped it on him if he hadn't. She jerked her head. "So what's with the chart on the Shumagins?"

His face lit up. For a moment the desire to share his news with someone, anyone, warred with the awareness of who he was talking to, but eagerness won out in the end. "I was looking for Sanak and Unga."

"Why?"

"Because I was reading this book about the Aleutians, and there's a story in it about a boat race back in the thirties or thereabouts. A boat race between a hundred-twenty-five-foot steamer and a kayak."

He beamed at her, blue eyes expectant beneath tousled blond hair, and dutifully she said, "A steamer and a kayak? No kidding? What happened?"

"The kayak won!" The announcement was delivered with all the air of an eyewitness to the event.

Kate expressed suitable astonishment, and he needed no

further urging to disgorge the whole story. "The steamer put in at Sanak to offload cargo, see, and these four Aleut guys came up in a kayak and challenged the captain of the steamer to a race." Andy's lip curled. "He wouldn't do it until they bet him a hundred dollars they could win."

"Easy money," she observed. She thought she caught a glimpse of an island off to starboard, but a tardy wisp of fog obscured it almost as soon as she saw it, and she settled back in the chair, listening to Andy with half an ear.

"That's what *he* thought," Andy said, his scorn immense and magnificent. "The steamer took off, and the kayak just sat there, and everybody onshore started hooting and laughing, but the Aleuts were waiting, counting the waves for the right wave, what they called the ninth wave. When it came along, they paddled to catch it and balanced themselves on top of it, and then they rode it, all the way to Unga! Before the trip was half over, they were out of the steamer's sight!" The beam was back. "First surfers north of the fifty-three! God, don't you just love Alaska!"

"Hitchhiking on a wave," Kate said. "I like it. Did the *Starr*'s skipper pay up?"

Andy nodded vigorously. "Uh-huh. He was a good sport."

"Good for him. More coffee?"

"Wait a minute." Andy paused, mug outstretched. "Did I say the steamer's name was the *Starr*?"

"Sure you did." The can of Carnation Evaporated Milk was empty but for a few drops. Kate sighed.

"No, I didn't," he said. "You already knew it. You already heard that story."

She looked over at his accusing expression. "About a thousand times," she admitted, a slow smile spreading across her face.

He didn't know whether to take offense or not, and as the decision hung in the balance Kate played her trump card. "I'm an Aleut myself, Andy. I think the first time my foster father told me that story I was four years old."

Andy stared at her, eyes and mouth three round, astonished O's. "Gosh," he breathed. "You're an Aleut? A real live Aleut?"

Kate kept her face straight with an effort. "A real live Aleut. Now be a good guy and go get me another can of milk for my coffee, okay? And toss the empty while you're at it."

She handed the can to him. He took it automatically, his eyes still wide and fixed on her face. "Have you ever paddled a kayak?"

"Never in my life," she said, and took him by the shoulders to turn him around and give him a firm shove in the direction of the stairs.

● ● ●

They made Dutch that evening. The harbor was crowded with crabbers, and their turn to unload didn't come until the following morning. The crew suited up in rain gear while Harry brought the *Avilda* around to the processor's dock. Working both booms on the dock and with all four of the deck crew in the hold loading brailers they had the old girl emptied out in less than two hours.

Harry shinnied up the ladder to the dock, reappearing in the galley half an hour later. "How much?" Andy said, his young voice excited. "What kind of price did we get?"

The skipper made a show of consulting the fish ticket he held in one hand. "Buck-fifty."

"A dollar and fifty cents?" Andy said. "Per crab?"

"Per *pound*," Kate corrected him gently.

Andy's voice went up into a squeak. "Per pound? Per *pound?*"

He lunged for paper and pencil. His face screwed up with concentration, the tip of his tongue protruding from one corner of his mouth. After tremendous amounts of scribbling and adding and erasing and multiplying, he produced a figure and stared down at it with disbelieving eyes. "Eighty-three hundred dollars?" he said finally. His face paled, flushed and paled again beneath its tan. Again his voice went up to a squeak. "A crew share for this one trip is *eighty-three hundred dollars?*"

Kate smacked him on the back. "If it was easy, everybody'd be doing it. That's why they pay us the big bucks, boy."

She looked around for agreement and found it, in a mild sort of way. Seth gave a casual nod, Ned said "uh-huh" in an absentminded tone, and Harry disappeared into his stateroom.

A little deflated, Andy turned to Kate. "For crying out loud, you'd think they made eighty-three hundred bucks every *day* out there."

"Yes," Kate said, "you would think that, wouldn't you." She picked up the piece of paper and peered at the clumsy squiggles. She made a few doodles with the pencil and totaled them up.

"Eighty-three hundred dollars?"

She nodded, her face wearing a rueful expression he didn't understand but was too wrought up to question. "Yup. It's eighty-three hundred dollars, all right. Each." Laying pencil and paper aside, she rubbed her face with both hands, hard. "Eighty-three hundred dollars," she repeated in a thoughtful voice. "Not bad for eight days' work."

Jack Morgan might live after all.

In one of those impetuous changes of mind for which Aleutian weather is rightfully famed, the fog shifted and revealed a high, broken overcast and, if Kate was not mistaken, a pale, brief and wholly transitory gleam that might be sunshine. The resulting scene was somewhere between appalling and enthralling. Dutch Harbor was a sheltered piece of Iliuliuk Bay, nuzzled up against Amaknak Island behind a mile-long spit of sand and gravel and grass. Amaknak Island, four miles long and a mile wide, in turn lay snugly within two arms of the much larger Unalaska Island, eighty-seven miles long and thirty-seven miles wide and the second largest in the Aleutian Chain. Amaknak Island looked like a pelican facing northeast, Unalaska like a tomahawk with the blade facing north-northwest. Mount Ballyhoo formed the beak of Amaknak's pelican, so named, Kate dimly remembered from some long-ago lesson in Mr. Kaufman's sixth-grade geography class, by Jack London when he'd been sealing between the Aleutians and the Kuriles at the turn of the century. That voyage had formed the basis for local color in *The Sea Wolf*, which Mr. Kaufman had forced down the class's collectively unwilling educational maw. All Kate could remember of the story was her conviction that though Humphrey Van Weyden might have survived Wolf Larsen, he wouldn't have lasted five minutes in the Park.

Ballyhoo had been her first sight of Dutch. In fact when she saw it loom up in the window of the 727 she flew in on she had been certain it was going to be her last sight of anything at all, as the airstrip clung precariously to a very narrow strip of land between the southwestern slopes of Ballyhoo (or the back of the pelican's head) and the Bering Sea. From the maps she knew a five-hundred-foot bridge connected Amaknak with Unalaska, and on the island of Unalaska was the village of Unalaska. Somewhere off to the northwest in the surrounding clouds was 6,680-foot Makushin Volcano, the second largest in the Chain. It was still active, as were most of the volcanoes in the Pacific's Ring of Fire. Kate tried not to think about it.

From nowhere on either island was there a view that did not include a vast, unending expanse of water. In the north it was the Bering Sea; in the south, the Pacific Ocean. Both bodies of water were a constant reminder of what fueled Dutch Harbor. Dutch was a boom town and looked it. Prefabricated buildings crowded up against each other along narrow strips of beach, beaches that were themselves crowded between a landscape that rose suddenly and vertically with very few softening curves, and a sea that from one moment to the next varied in color from bright blue to dull green. Looking at this view was as alarming as it was invigorating, Kate now discovered, as if she were riding a roller coaster with both feet planted firmly on the ground.

Kate always felt better when she knew exactly where she was, and having identified all the relevant topographical features, she started out down the gravel road with a will. It was sodden beneath her feet. Gulls gave raucous screams as they swooped and dived overhead. A bald eagle perched on the top of a streetlight. He looked down his beak at her in the haughty manner of his kind, and after admiring him for a moment she passed on. The road was an obstacle course of fast-moving pickup trucks and vans, each of the vans with the logo of a different taxi service painted on their sides. Another interesting fact Andy had gleaned from his book on the Aleutians was that there were thirteen cab companies in Dutch, and within the first mile of her walk Kate had narrowly missed being run over by twelve of them.

She passed a crab processor, a surimi plant, another processor, another surimi plant, making her way down the gravel road that paralleled the beach and the rectangular harbor. She dodged a red Ford pickup with a SuperCab crammed with an indeterminate amount of people in bright yellow rain gear, and came upon a group of fishermen, identical in jeans, plaid shirts, shoepacs, navy-blue knit watch caps and unshaven faces. They stood in the middle of the road, oblivious to the trucks and vans rattling impatiently around them. They were all talking at once, at the tops of their voices, and punctuating their words with vociferous gesticulation. Kate paused to listen.

The man at the center of the group shook his head adamantly and held up ten fingers.

"Forget it!" one of the other men exclaimed. He had a dark, full beard that did little to conceal his choler. "Fifty and not a penny more!"

Kate, craning her neck, saw that the man at the center of the group had a bundle of loose fur beneath one arm. He held it up and it resolved itself into a hat, the kind seen in illustrations of winter life in Moscow. The fur was long and deep brown, almost black in color. The man showed it around the circle, allowing the prospective buyers to finger it admiringly. There were murmurs of appreciation at its softness and shine. Kate realized the scruffy guy must be off the big Russian processor anchored in the harbor, and was in the act of trying to raise some spending money. She elbowed forward for a closer look at the fur.

"Fifty," the fisherman who had bid last repeated.

The Russian, obdurate, shook his head and held up ten fingers again.

"Goddammit!" The fisherman was frustrated. A friend standing next to him said something in a low voice and he gave his head an impatient shake. "I forgot her birthday, I've gotta send her something or she'll throw all my clothes out the window like she did last time. She's into that ethnic shit, she'll love a Russian hat from a real Russian. Okay, sixty." He held up six fingers.

The Russian stood firm at a hundred. He couldn't speak a word of English but he knew a desperate man when he saw one. He was right; the fisherman eventually peeled five grimy twenties from a roll that would have choked a hippopotamus and exchanged them for the hat. Kate waited until the men had moved on before going to stand next to the Russian fisherman. "What kind of fur was it?" she asked.

He was counting his money, laboriously, licking his fingers between each bill. Unsatisfied with the first count, or perhaps disbelieving it, he counted a second time before looking up, his face split with an immense grin. It widened when he saw Kate, and he fired a stream of Russian in her direction.

She spread her hands and gave him a rueful smile that he had no problem interpreting and that left him undiscouraged. He pantomimed chugalugging a drink and looked at her hopefully, a big, rumpled, enthusiastic puppy dog. "Okay?" he said, evidently the limit of his English vocabulary.

What the hell, she thought. Might as well provide herself with some cover in case she ran into someone else off the *Avilda*. The prospect of meeting Jack with an enormous Russian in tow also had its appeal. "You know the Shipwreck?" she suggested out loud, and the Russian's grin threatened to split his face in two. It appeared he knew the Shipwreck. Kate smiled, shrugged and nodded.

Without further ado her new friend placed a massive and

proprietary arm around her shoulder and urged her down the road.

"Wait a minute," she said, holding up both hands. He halted, his face falling ludicrously. "No, it's okay, I'll go with you, I'm going that way anyway. But the hat." She demonstrated, pulling off her own, a baseball cap with the Niniltna Native Association logo stitched across the front. She pointed after the other fishermen, patted the canvas on her hat and rubbed her fingers together. "What was it made of? Your hat?"

He hesitated, looking at her.

"It's all right, I'm just curious," she assured him. "I do a little trapping myself. What was it?"

Still he hesitated. Kate wet her lips and gave him her best smile and his reservations dissolved. He looked around to make sure no one was looking, and held one hand at his side, palm down. "Woof," he said.

She laughed. "That's what I thought." She remembered Mutt and her smile faded, but he laughed back at her and offered his arm again. She took it. He would have steered her directly for the Shipwreck if she hadn't just as firmly steered him first to the Alyeska Trading Company, an all-purpose general store selling everything from California oranges to Stanley screwdrivers to Nikon cameras to Levi's jeans. Kate was there to buy dental floss but her Russian admirer took one look at the crowded shelves and fell in love, and Kate spent the next thirty minutes trailing after him up one aisle and down the next. He swooned over the coffee. He agonized over the relative merits of Marlboros and unfiltered Camels. Dismissing the best Timex had to offer with a decisive shake of his head, he was investigating the workings of a Canon Sure Shot when Kate looked up and saw Harry Gault over by

28

the meat counter, talking rapidly in a low voice to a short man with Asian features. He looked stubborn, Harry angry, and they both looked somehow furtive.

Kate had begun an unobtrusive drift in their direction when half a dozen of her new Russian friend's shipmates rolled in the door and engulfed the two of them. Harry looked up at the shouts and laughter. Caught looking at him, Kate met his eyes calmly and nodded hello. His eyebrows snapped together, he scowled and ushered the Asian man down an aisle and out of sight.

The Russians looked from Kate to their shipmate and back again and there was a considerable wagging of eyebrows and a lot of talk recognizable as ribald in any language. One of them asked her a question. Of course it meant nothing to her and she shook her head helplessly. Her newfound bosom buddy held up one finger in inspiration and poked himself in the chest. "Anatoly! Anatoly!"

"You're Anatoly," she said, nodding. He pointed at her and waited. "Kate. I'm Kate."

He looked puzzled for a moment. "Kate?" Dawn broke. "Ekaterina!" She nodded, and jumped when the entire crew shouted her name with one voice, causing heads to turn all over the store. Anatoly, noticing her alarmed expression, grabbed her hand and hauled her over to the window. He pointed at the processor anchored in the harbor, a squat, ungraceful ship that towered over its harbor mates, looking like an immense gray gull with its head tucked beneath one wing. "Ekaterina!" He pointed from the boat to Kate and back again. "Ekaterina! Ekaterina!"

"Ekaterina!" his shipmates yelled, beaming at her.

A light went on over Kate's head. "You mean your boat's name is Ekaterina, too?"

He nodded excitedly. "Ekaterina! Ekaterina!"

"Well, it's nice to meet you, *Ekaterina,*" she said to the boat, "and you, too, Anatoly." She held out her hand.

He was at least six feet tall and seemed six feet wide, so when he put his hands on her upper arms and lifted her without seeming effort she was unsurprised, if a bit startled. He kissed her, great smacking kisses on both cheeks and mouth, before setting her back down on her feet. There was a cheer from his shipmates and Kate could feel herself flushing, but she had to laugh. "Well, thank you. Nice to meet you, too. I think."

Eventually Anatoly decided on a Sony boombox and a selection of Top Ten cassette tapes, leaving Kate to wonder how Hammer was going to go over in Magadan. With the boombox clutched firmly beneath one arm and Kate beneath his other, Anatoly plotted a course for the door, followed by laughing, chattering shipmates similarly laden with packages. Kate felt like she was leading a parade. As they exited the store, what looked like an entire ship's company of Japanese fishermen flooded in and headed straight for the meat counter. So that was why everything in the store was priced in yen, too, Kate thought, and wondered why the store's owners didn't price their products in rubles as well.

• • •

The Shipwreck Bar had been a Dutch watering hole for time immemorial, which at this longitude meant since at least before World War II. A cargo ship for Alaska Steam, she'd been conscripted by General Samuel Buckner to supply troops rushed to the Aleutians following Pearl Harbor. A gale drove her ashore during her first year of service. The SeaBees restored her to an upright position, filled her hold with concrete for ballast, reconditioned her generator and used her for a barracks during the war. Abandoned for two decades, when the crab fishing picked up in the sixties a local businessman acquired her as government surplus and remodeled her into a restaurant, hotel and bar.

Double doors were cut into the side of the hull. Kate entered first, only to dodge back out of the way of a fisherman slow dancing with a bar stool, eyes closed and cheek to seat. Jimmy Buffet was wishing he had a pencil-thin mustache and about thirty fishermen were crowded around the jukebox, leaning up against it and each other and singing along in an enthusiastic if tuneless chorus. Grimy windows cut through the hull looked out over the docks and boats of the harbor, tables were scattered around the room with a lavish hand, the floor was filthy with spilled beer and cigarette butts, and Kate couldn't even see the bar with all the bodies crowded up against it. Her eyes becoming accustomed to the gloom, she conservatively estimated about one woman for every twelve men in the place. She further estimated that at thirty-one years of age she was by far the oldest person in the room, save perhaps the bartender. He was a wrinkled little man with an anxious expression between the creases, who seemed to be the only waiter and was in constant motion between bar and tables.

One of those tables became free and Anatoly and his shipmates herded their prize female across the room in a proprietary manner that made Kate feel like the single houri in a harem otherwise filled with very needy sheiks. A chair was produced and she got to sit in it for all of thirty seconds before Anatoly had her out on the dance floor. He was promptly cut in on by one of his friends, and he by a third,

31

and so on. They rotated her through the entire crew several times and what had to have been most of the jukebox's repertoire before Kate, flushed and laughing, protested. Anatoly, her current partner, became all concern and ushered her solicitously back to her chair, its current occupant removed by the scruff of his neck. Anatoly rattled off something to his shipmates and there was a concerted rush to the bar. Almost instantaneously on the table before her appeared a Michelob, a Rainier, an Olympia, three shot glasses brimming with a clear liquid and one mixed drink with a slice of pineapple hooked over one side of the glass and a tiny pink paper parasol draped over the other.

Kate looked from the drinks to her escorts. "Thank you, but—"

Anatoly said firmly, "*Spasiba*."

"I beg your pardon."

"'Dank you,' *nyet*," he said. "*Spasiba*."

"Oh. I see." Kate waved a hand over the table and said, "*Spasiba*, then, *spasiba* very much, but I don't drink." She pointed at the assorted glasses and bottles and back to herself, all the while shaking her head from side to side. "I don't drink." She couldn't help laughing at their crestfallen faces. With a firm hand she moved each drink to a place more or less in front of one of them and before any of them could beat her to it rose to her feet in search of something tall, cold and nonalcoholic.

"Hi, honey," some jerk at the next table smirked. He patted his lap suggestively. "Have a seat." She ignored him, and someone jerkier seated next to him growled, "Got something against Americans, girlie?" She ignored him, too, only to be brought up short against a barrel chest clad in brilliant orange and green plaid wool. She took a deep breath and looked up, prepared to defend her virtue at all costs, only to encounter a pair of mild brown eyes in a moon-shaped face. "Name the Beach Boys," he demanded.

"I—what?"

"Name the Beach Boys," he repeated. He swayed a little on his feet. There wasn't room enough for him to fall down, for which Kate was profoundly grateful.

"The Beach Boys," she said. "Well, there was Mike Love, and the Wilson brothers—"

"Which one's still dead?"

"'Still dead?'"

The moon face looked disapproving. "What's the matter, I don't speak English good enough for you? Which Beach Boy's still dead?"

Kate offered him a conciliatory smile. "I'm sorry. I don't know which one's still dead."

The moon-faced man huffed out an impatient sigh. "Don't anyone in this bar know nothing about the legends of our own time? Jesus!" He looked back at Kate and said with exaggerated patience, "D for Dennis. D for dead. Simple. Get it?"

"Got it," Kate said solemnly.

"D for Dennis. D for dead." The moon face crumpled and a tear ran down his cheek. "Goddammit."

It was like that all the way across the bar, and the journey took time and persistence and some strong elbow work. When she finally got through she could see why. She stood stiff and still, barely breathing.

Someone had dribbled a thin line of white powder on the bar, a line that extended the entire twenty-foot length of the scarred wood. About one fisherman per inch was snorting it up through straws, thin glass tubes and rolled-up hundred-dollar bills with all the finesse of a bunch of enthusiastic hogs working their way through a cornucopian trough.

Kate was not exactly a virgin when it came to understanding the effects of rash and reckless youth combined with too much money, but this blatant display was something even beyond her ken. As she stood there, stunned, an amused voice drawled, "Like a toot, little lady?"

She turned to see a man with a grin like a hungry shark standing next to her, and she remained so astounded that he mistook her silence for interest. An expansive sweep of one arm took in the bar. "Go ahead, the party's on me." He looked her over with a predatory eye. What he saw must have pleased him, for he gave the bulging bag in front of him a possessive pat, grinned that shark's grin again and said, "Plenty more where this came from. Maybe we can work out a little something in trade?"

A deep voice said, "I don't think so."

Jack Morgan was tall, six feet two inches, and he was broad, well over two hundred pounds, but what gave the shark pause was the expression on his almost ugly face. It might have been the broad, unsmiling mouth, or the high-bridged nose already broken more than once, or the cold, clear, steady blue of his eyes, narrowed slightly against the cigarette smoke that swirled and eddied across the room like the Aleutian fog offshore. He stood where he was, waiting, like a rock indifferent to the roughest surf, and he looked at the shark, calm, watchful and without a trace of apprehension.

The shark was clearly taken aback by all this sangfroid but he was game. "Why don't we let the little lady speak for herself?"

"Because she's already spoken for," Jack said, just as smoothly. He looked at Kate and quirked an eyebrow, daring her to react. Little pleased as she was by his high-handedness, still less did she want to start a fight. Already noise was dying down around them as fishermen became aware of the confrontation and downed bottles and straws to watch avidly to see what happened next. She caught a glimpse of Ned Nordhoff toward the back of the crowd and that decided her. She gave Jack a silent nod and stepped to his side. He rested a casual but unmistakably possessive hand on her shoulder, gave the shark an amiable smile and raised his voice. "Barkeep!"

The bartender left off rewashing a perfectly clean glass and bustled down. "What'll you have?"

Jack jerked his head. "A room."

The bartender gave Kate a speculative look and Jack a lascivious grin. When no answering grin was forthcoming his own faded and he said nervously, "That'll be a hundred bucks. Cash. Up front."

"All right." Unperturbed, Jack produced a money clip and peeled off two fifties and handed them over. "When's checkout time?"

"Checkout time?"

Jack was patient. "What time in the morning do we have to be out?"

The bartender gaped. "You mean you're staying all night?"

For the first time Jack looked a little wary. "That was the idea. Is there a problem?"

"You want a whole room for one whole *night*?" Jack nodded. "What the hell you going to be doing up there that'll take all night?"

It was so obviously shock rather than prurient interest that prompted the question that Jack said only, "How about a key?"

The bartender woke from his self-induced trance. "The

whole night'll cost you more than a hundred, I can tell you that, pardner."

Unmoved, Jack said, "How much more?"

Taken aback, the bartender glanced around for help. "I don't know," he admitted, "no one's ever asked for a whole room for the whole night before."

Jack reached for his money clip and peeled another hundred off. "That do?" The bartender looked dazedly down at the bills in his outstretched hand, and Jack sighed and added another hundred. The bartender swallowed hard, the bills disappeared into a pocket and he said, "I'll get that key."

Conversation picked up as they followed him up the gangway bolted to the back wall. Kate's last sight of the bar was of Anatoly's enormous brown eyes, swimming with reproach, following her every step of the way.

• • •

The room wasn't much bigger than the stateroom Kate was sharing with Andy on the *Avilda*, and but for the bunkbeds looked very similar. The bulkheads were metal and cool to the touch, the bunk was narrow and built in to the wall with drawers beneath it and a porthole above, and the adjoining head was the size of an aspidistra planter. "Hold it," Kate said when the bartender would have left them. Pulling back the covers on the bed, she sniffed the sheets. They smelled fresh and they looked clean. So did the toilet, and when she pulled back the shower curtain the floor looked fungi-free. It was far more than she'd hoped for. She reentered the room and nodded at Jack, who repeated, "So, when do you want us out of here?"

The bartender scratched his head. "Hell, I don't know."

"When's your boat due out?" Jack asked Kate.

She shrugged. "We're waiting on a part they're flying in from Anchorage. Could be one day. Could be two."

"But it won't be tomorrow." She shook her head, and Jack looked back at the bartender, who threw up his hands. "The hell with it," he told them, "stay as long as you like. And don't even *think* about complaining about the noise. This ain't exactly the Holiday Inn, you know."

"We know," Jack said dryly, and the bartender stamped out.

• • •

"Did you see that line of coke?" Kate demanded as soon as the door slammed shut behind him. Jack nodded. "God knows I'm no prude, Jack, but Jesus! There had to be thousands of dollars worth of hits on that bar!"

He unzipped his jacket and sat down to unlace his boots. "Hundreds of thousands."

"Enough for Amaknak Island to achieve lift-off," she said, her torn voice outraged. "I'd bet my last dime there wasn't a kid there over twenty-five, and every last one of them due to go back out into the Bering Sea as soon as their boats are refueled. You've got to do something."

"Look, Kate, I don't mean to sound unfeeling," he said, grunting a little as the first boot came off, "but could we concentrate for a minute on why you're here?"

"You've got to do something," she reiterated.

He set the second boot beside the first, lining the two up with meticulous precision. "Kate. I'm an investigator for the Anchorage D.A. I am not a police officer, and even if I were this isn't anywhere remotely near my jurisdiction."

She told him what he could do with his jurisdiction, and he

said, "You want me to wade into that crowd of drunks, most of them just off their boats, thousands of dollars in their pockets, thousands of miles from home and family, roaring to have a good time, and tell them they can't?" He snorted. "There wouldn't be enough of me left to lick up off the floor."

"Then call the cops! Call the troopers! Call the DEA!"

"You think they aren't already here?"

She glared at him, impotent.

He waved a hand in the general direction of the airstrip. "Three different public air carriers fly into Dutch every day. Ma and Pa Kettle can fly in for the price of a ticket, seven hundred dollars round-trip if they buy in advance. So can Joe Fisherman. And so can Joe Blow, your friendly neighborhood pusher." He saw her expression and his own softened. "Kate. Some of these kids are pulling down five, ten grand a trip. It's cold work, it's boring, it's lonely, and for most of them it's the toughest job they'll ever have. Oh," he said, holding up a hand palm out when she would have spoken, "the cops and the troopers and the DEA'll do their best, like they always do, understaffed and underfunded and with the entire fishing community closing ranks against them. But it all comes down to the same thing in the end, escape for sale. Here, who can resist that kind of sales pitch?"

Her glare was damning and maybe even a little righteous. "I can."

His grin was tired but appreciative. "That's why I love you, Katie, you tough little broad, you. Now what have you got for me?"

"Zip," she said with relish.

He leaned back in his chair, crossed his feet on the edge of the bunk, laced his hands behind his head and looked at her, waiting.

She blew out an exasperated breath and flopped on the bunk, kicking off her boots. "What did you expect? You fly into the Park with some cockamamie story about the Case of the Disappearing Crewmen, and yank me out of there so fast I barely have time to get Mutt and her pups over to Mandy's. The next thing I know I'm on a boat in the middle of the Boring Sea, in gale-force winds and freezing rain, pulling pots and wondering what the hell I'm doing there."

"You didn't have to come," he pointed out. "As you have made abundantly clear on more than one occasion, you don't work for me anymore."

"Yeah, yeah, yeah," she said. Jack was being reasonable and Kate wasn't interested in reasonable at the moment. "Except for when you offer me four hundred dollars a day and expenses." Not to mention $8,300 a week in incidental earnings, she thought. The prospect cheered her, but she would be damned before she let him see it.

"Besides," he added, "the *Avilda* needed a deckhand pronto, and the board couldn't stall off Gault forever, not with so many wanna-be deckhands in Dutch. There wasn't time to brief you."

"There's time now," she pointed out.

He eyed the bunk, and her on it. "I was kind of hoping we could try out that bunk first." He waggled his eyebrows. "It's going to be tough, justifying it on my expense account. I want to make sure I'm getting my money's worth."

She bit back a smile and said sternly, "Get on with it."

He gave a mournful sigh and dug into his pack, producing a tattered, bulging file folder with sheets of paper sliding out in every direction. "I assumed when I flew into the Park last week that you had heard of the two crewmen who were lost last March."

"Don't assume anything of the kind. The Park's not on a paper route, I don't have a satellite dish, or a television, for that matter, and I only listen to National Public Radio. Or I do when the skip is right, which isn't often, and Bob Edwards doesn't talk a lot about Alaska anyway. And besides, you and I were busy with other matters last spring." Unconsciously, Kate rubbed at her right shoulder, feeling again the kick of the shotgun as she faced down a man with ten bodies, two of them children, littering the Park behind him. Lottie she refused to think about at all.

"True." Jack's voice was without inflection, but he took care not to look at her.

"Start from the beginning, and don't worry about repeating yourself. I want to hear it all this time."

"All right." He made a stab at shaking the mass of paperwork in his lap into some kind of order, and gave it up as a lost cause. Tilting his chair back against the bulkhead, he closed his eyes and recited from memory.

"The *Avilda* is one of a fleet of deep-sea fishing boats owned by a consortium of fishing families from Freetown, Oregon, called Alaska Ventures, Inc. They've been smart and successful, and they've built up quite a sizable fleet over the last forty years." He pawed through the folder and by a miracle found what he was looking for near the top of the file. "There's the *Avilda*, your boat. There's the *Lady Killigrew,* the *Madame Ching,* the—"

Kate sat up, and he looked at her. "What?"

The names triggered a memory somewhere, but she couldn't immediately track it down. She shook her head. "Nothing. Never mind."

He looked at her for a moment longer, decided it wasn't worth the effort and returned to his list. "There's the *Mary*

Read, the *Anne Bonney* and a sixth on the ways at Marco, the—"

Kate's memory clicked in and a wide grin spread across her face. "Let me guess. The *Grace O'Malley*."

He examined his list again. "No, the *Mary Lovell*." Kate laughed out loud. "What?"

She was still chuckling, but she shook her head. "Nothing. Never mind. It's not important."

Jack mistrusted the smug expression on her face but shrugged his shoulders and looked back down at his list. "The fleet spends summers in Freetown, refitting, maintenance and repairs, upgrading equipment, that kind of thing. Winters, they spend fishing in Alaska, out of Kodiak or Dutch Harbor, always for crab, *opilio*, *bairdi*, red and blue king. Lately there's been some talk of refitting a few of the vessels for bottom fishing, but Alaska Ventures' board of directors seems to feel that bottom fishing is going to be severely curtailed in the near future."

"They *are* smart," Kate observed. "A lot of marine biologists blame bottom fishing for the drop in king crab stocks in the mid-eighties, and they lobby hard in Juneau and Washington. They've got the tree huggers on their side, too. Hard to buck. What's any of this got to do with the Case of the Disappearing Crewmen?"

"I'm getting to that. As you know, the *Avilda* is skippered by Harry Gault. During the tail end of last season, Gault used the *Avilda* to haul a barge from Kodiak to Dutch Harbor. The barge belonged to the processor Alaska Ventures delivers to, so he was doing them a favor. Not much of one, as it turned out."

"What happened?"

"It is generally agreed, if not said right out loud, that

through bad weather and bad seamanship Gault lost the barge."

"Lost the barge?"

Jack nodded. "The line parted twice before he finally lost it for good the third time. They spent a lot of time going around in circles trying to find it. No luck. In the meantime, they ran out of water."

"Ran out of water?"

Jack nodded. "Ran out of water." When Kate would have said more he held up one hand and cautioned, "Remember, the deck boss and the remaining deckhand backed him up on this."

"Ned Nordhoff and Seth Skinner."

Jack nodded again. "So he drove the boat over to the nearest island, anchored, and the other crew members"—Jack fumbled impatiently with the pile of paper in his lap— "doggone it, okay, here it is—their names were Christopher Alcala and Stuart Brown—went ashore to look for water."

The faces of the two young crewmen appeared again before Kate's eyes. "Went ashore where?"

"Ah, what, the island's name was Anua."

"Got a map?"

Jack fished around in his daypack and tossed a folded piece of paper over to her. She flattened it on the bunk and found the little island halfway down the chain, ringed in a circle of black Marksalot she had no difficulty in identifying as Jack's handiwork. Jack had always leaned toward black Marksalot for notes, arrows and marginal balloons on any piece of evidence that was write-onable, to the vocal disgust of the district attorneys who had then to introduce the evidence into the trial record. "What's on it? On Anua, I mean?"

"An airstrip dating back to World War II, an active volcano. That's about it. Pretty standard for an Aleutian island."

Kate measured the air miles between Dutch Harbor and Anua, her brows puckered. "Mmm."

He waited, but that was all she said. "Alcala and Brown left the *Avilda* at about four in the afternoon, in the skiff. They had a flashlight and a bunch of jerry cans."

"That all?"

"Uh-huh."

"No survival gear? No tent, no sleeping bags, not even matches?"

"According to Gault, they weren't anticipating spending the night."

"This was March?"

"Yeah."

"In the Aleutians?"

"Yeah."

Kate lay back down on the bunk. "Kind of gives new meaning to the word 'dumb,' don't it. What happened?"

"What you might expect, and remember this was the first trip north for both of them."

"First and last."

"Yeah. Anyway, according to Gault, Skinner and Nordhoff the skiff made it into shore, and then it started snowing. The crew on the boat lost sight of the island and the skiff. It socked in overnight. The next morning there were two inches of snow on the ground and no sight of skiff or crew."

"Did they go ashore to check?"

Jack shook his head. "No."

"What?"

"No, they didn't. They said they had no way to get there. The skiff was already ashore."

Still disbelieving, Kate demanded, "I presume they had a life raft?"

"Two of them." Jack grinned at her. "Gault says he didn't want to use them, in case he ran into trouble later on."

Kate stared at him. "And this is the good ship Lollipop you signed me onto? Thanks a whole bunch, Jack. So what happened next?"

"Gault called the Coast Guard."

Something in his voice made Kate say sharply, "How soon?"

"From the Coast Guard logs it was noon the day of the disappearance before Gault got around to calling them." He looked up with a bland expression. "He ran the *Avilda* up and down and around the island, looking for signs of life through the binoculars. When he couldn't find any, he pulled the hook and set course for Dutch."

Kate was speechless. Jack's smile was bland. "It gets better. When the Coast Guard fired up a chopper and took a run out there, it seems that Gault had given them the wrong coordinates, so they searched the wrong part of the island."

When Kate found her voice it was only for a very weak, "You're kidding me."

"Nope. The Coasties didn't discover this until a couple of weeks later, when the operator who took the call compared notes with the pilot. So they went out again. Didn't find anything that time, either."

"Nothing at all?"

"Nope."

"Not even a jerry can? An oar? A hat or a glove? Nothing?"

"Nothing." Jack refiled the list of boat names in the folder, just missing losing the entire mass on the floor.

"Why the hell hasn't Gault been fired?" Kate demanded.

Jack smiled. "Because Captain Harry Gault had the forethought to marry a daughter of one of Alaska Ventures' board of directors. Just last January, in fact."

Kate folded her hands behind her head and stared at the ceiling. After a moment, she said thoughtfully, "How very *strategic* of him."

"The guy is slick," Jack admitted. "And of course, no one has been able to prove otherwise, Skinner and Nordhoff back Gault up, so no charges have been filed."

"But."

"But," Jack agreed. "The board of Alaska Ventures is as nervous as a cat with two tails in a room full of rocking chairs."

"Alcala and Brown have family?"

Jack bestowed an approving smile on her. "Yes, they do, and they want to know what happened, and they're starting to get loud about it. Marine insurance is not exactly cheap or easy to come by, so the board of Alaska Ventures has begun a little discreet investigation of Harry Gault's past."

"And now the state's getting into the act."

"You and me, babe."

She twisted her head to stare at him. "What's this 'you and *me* babe' crap? I don't see you out on the deck of the *Avilda*, soaking wet and freezing cold and up to your ass in tanner crab." And puking your guts up over the rail every five minutes, she could have added, but didn't.

Jack managed to look hurt. "You're the one with the fishing experience."

"Fishing for salmon in Prince William Sound and a couple of months fishing for king crab out of Kodiak isn't quite the same thing as trying to drown myself in the Boring goddam Sea," she retorted. "I can't believe I let you talk me into this. The *Aleutians*. In *October*. I must be out of my mind."

"You never did answer me. About why you did come. I would have lost money betting you wouldn't."

"Why'd the bear go round the mountain?" She shrugged. "I've never been on the Peninsula, or seen the Aleutians. I could never afford the airfare."

Unconvinced, Jack let it slide. "So. Tell me about the good ship *Avilda* and her happy crew."

Kate looked back at the ceiling. "She's a good ship, all right, or she would be if someone took the time to take care of her. She deserves a better crew than those assholes."

"All of them are assholes?"

Kate thought back to her first day on board. Harry, his face congested with suppressed rage, had shouted at her. "Nordensen says I gotta hire you, okay. But I don't like women, and I don't like Injuns, and I especially don't like Injun women on board my ship, they're nothing but trouble. You stay out of the guys' pants, you hear?" He'd shaken his fist in her face, practically frothing at the mouth. "You fuck one of us, you fuck us all, you understand? Any trouble between the guys over you and you're off the goddam boat!" He'd leered at poor Andy, who had blushed beet red beneath his tan and hung his head.

Kate, unperturbed, had given Harry a cool nod. "I heard you the first time."

In truth, she felt Harry had done her a favor with the blunt announcement. All or none? That was fine with Kate. Harry Gault wasn't much of a sailor or a fisherman, but he understood the dynamics of a cramped and isolated workplace. So far, neither Ned nor Seth, nor Harry for that matter, had made any moves in her direction. There'd been a few leers and some crude remarks, but no pawing, and from her last fishing experience she knew how fortunate she was.

"They're men," she told Jack. "They're fishermen. They're crab fishermen. And they're *Alaskan* crab fishermen. Of course they're assholes." She thought, and added, a trifle reluctantly, "Except maybe for Andy, my bunkie."

Jack sat very still. "You're bunking with a guy?"

Kate raised an eyebrow in his direction. "Don't go all Neanderthal on me, Jack. He's just a kid, and from California at that. The kind of guy who thinks the New Age arrived with the invention of the fast forward button on the VCR remote."

The amusement in her voice when she spoke, warm and somewhat rueful, was not reassuring. "What about Skinner and Nordhoff?"

"Too soon to say, but they're in tight with Gault," Kate said. "They hardly talk to Andy or me outside of work."

"And Gault?"

Kate gave a short, unamused laugh. "For the health of every fisherman afloat on the Pacific Ocean, Harry Gault should shoulder an oar and walk inland until he finds someone who doesn't know what it is and stay there for the rest of his life."

"Umm," Jack said, who had never considered poetry necessary, and who was more interested in the way Kate tucked her hair behind her left ear anyway. "What did you pull down, this trip?" he asked idly, gaze on that left ear.

"The usual crew share. Eight percent of the gross."

"Which was?"

"Eighty-three hundred bucks."

His eyes widened. "Wow. Eighty-three hundred? For eight days work?" He gave a respectful whistle. "Hell, that's, what, that's almost eleven hundred a day, isn't it?" She nodded. "Wow," he said again. "Marry me and support me in the style in which I intend to become accustomed."

She stretched out her inconsiderable length in one long, lazy reach. She fluttered her eyelashes and patted the bunk. "Mmm, I don't know. Let me review your application one more time."

She didn't have to ask him twice.

CHAPTER 3

THEY ROSE EARLY THE next morning, hungry from no dinner the night before, and went looking for a restaurant. Over breakfast at the Unisea Restaurant, equally beguiled by the eggs Benedict and the view of the old submarine dock, Kate said impulsively, "Let's fly out there."

"Out where?" Jack said around a mouthful of Canadian bacon.

"Anua." Kate waved a hand at the clear sky. "It'd be flying in the face of Providence not to take advantage of that, so let's fly out there and take a look for ourselves. You have got Cecily with you, right? You're supposed to be caribou hunting and sight-seeing, you must have brought her along."

He swallowed. "How far is it?"

"If that map you gave me last night is accurate, I figure about a hundred and sixty miles from Dutch."

"Hmm." He studied the ceiling and chewed, figuring. "Shouldn't take us more than an hour and twenty minutes, each way, and we'll have fuel to spare, just in case. I suppose we could."

"Please? I'd like to see for myself the place where whatever the hell it was happened, happened."

He wiped his mouth with a paper napkin. "Let me check with Flight Service on the forecast. If the weather's with us, we'll do it."

49

• • •

After breakfast Kate left Jack to check in with the *Avilda*. Nordhoff, Skinner and Gault were all off somewhere, leaving Andy on watch. "Hey, Kate!" he called across the boats between the *Avilda* and the boat slip. "And where were you last night, little girl?"

"None of your business," she told him sweetly. "We still leaving tomorrow morning?"

He nodded. "If that part comes in. The skipper doesn't seem to be in much of a hurry."

"Good," Kate said, although she wondered why, after such a successful run, Harry Gault wasn't hot to get hot on the crab again.

"Look what I got!" Andy said, delving into his coat pocket and producing a small object wrapped in butcher paper. He unfolded the paper with exquisite care and displayed the object therein with immense pride.

Kate looked and saw a small rectangular lump of what might have been ivory, carved into the very rough image of a fat, smiling little Buddha. "A *billiken*," she said. "'As a good luck bringer, I'm a honey, to bring good luck, just rub my tummy.'"

"Oh, you know the verse!" Andy said, disappointed. "This guy came by and asked me if I wanted to buy it. He didn't want to sell it because it had been in his family for six generations, but he was broke and needed the airfare to get home. I didn't want to buy it like that, a family antique and all, but what could I do? The guy said I'd be doing him a favor."

With a superhuman effort Kate refrained from asking how much the guy had charged him for the figurine, and with still another superhuman effort did not tell Andy that *billikens* had not appeared on the Alaskan scene until the Klondike Gold Rush in 1899 brought the first Orientals into the Yukon and some sourdough thought up the *billiken* in Buddha's image. She even managed to refrain from asking how someone could just "wander" by the fourth boat in a raft, and was justifiably proud of herself and her restraint.

"Isn't Alaska just the greatest place?" Andy said, beaming. Fortunately it was a rhetorical question and Kate was not required to answer. "Oh, I almost forgot. Want your check?" He handed her a slip of paper.

"Well, since it's here." She examined the figures written on it, her mouth pulled into a wry expression. $8,300. Eighty-three hundred smackeroos. Eight thousand three hundred dollars in legal tender for all debts, public and private. No matter how many times she read it, it came out the same.

Yes indeed, Jack Morgan just might live after all. Folding the check carefully, she tucked it into her pocket and went down to her stateroom for a change of clothes.

Andy watched quizzically when she reemerged on deck and started back across the railing. "Where are you off to now?"

She flashed a grin at him. "Got a date."

● ● ●

He cast his eyes heavenward. "Ask a stupid question."

After extensive research and careful study of the resulting data, the National Oceanic and Atmospheric Administration has decreed that on average there are only eight days of sunshine per year in the Aleutian Islands. This day, midway through October, usually the first month of the storm season, was, incredibly, one of them. The storm that had blown the *Avilda* back to Dutch had blown out again, and on its heels was a high pressure system that stretched as high, wide and handsome as they could see in every direction. The view from five thousand feet up was spectacular.

"I don't believe this," Kate said over her headset.

"Don't believe what?" Jack said. He barely cradled the yoke in one large fist, his feet relaxed on the pedals. There was no turbulence, and Cecily the Cessna sailed smoothly down the Aleutian sky for all the world like a Cadillac sailing down a freshly paved section of interstate.

"I don't believe that, for one thing," she said, pointing to Jack's relaxed grip. "I don't believe you're steering this crate with one finger."

His look was of mild surprise. "Why not?"

"This is *October*," she replied. "This is the *Aleutians*. This kind of weather doesn't happen in October in the Aleutians. From what I've heard and read, this kind of weather hardly ever happens here at all, during any time of the year. You should hear fishermen talking about the Aleutians when they're back home. The winds alone, the williwaws—they call this place the Cradle of the Winds, did you know that? All my life, listening to those guys' stories, I've thought this place was some kind of hellhole. But look at it," she said with a sweep of her hand, her tone caught between astonishment and awe. "Just look at it."

The islands strung out before them, as far as they could see, in a long, slow, southwesterly curve. The white peaks glowed against the deep blue of the sea, like a string of pearls draped across a shell of blue-tinted mother-of-pearl in a jeweler's window. Each island had its own volcano, rising steeply to tickle at the belly of the sky, and most of them were smoking or steaming or both. The cones were smoothed over with termination dust, which began near the summit of each mountain in a heavy layer of frozen icing, thinning out to a scant layer of vanilla frosting nearer the shoreline. The snow did not so much soften the islands' rugged outlines as it emphasized them. Beneath it, in dramatic shifts of shadow and sunlight, every island was a rough and tumble surge of magmatic rock, thrust violently up from the bowels of mother earth to plunge four and five and six thousand feet and more straight down into the sea. In those topographical entrails could be read the history of the planet.

"It's like watching the earth being born," Kate said softly. "I've never seen anything like it."

Jack looked as satisfied as if he'd arranged for the Aleutians to be where they were, the day to be as clear as it was and for the *Avilda* to break down just when it did, all to get Kate in the air at this place, at this time, in his company. For the next two hours they forgot they were on their way to the scene of the mysterious disappearance of two ship's crewmen, and played at sight-seeing and rubber-necking in the best tradition of the American tourist. They flew low over a brief stretch of sand littered with the green glass balls Japanese fishermen use for net floats. They annoyed a herd of walrus sunbathing on another beach, until a bull in the crowd, a magnificent old beast with tusks two feet long, reared up and roared at them, daring them to come on down. Off the shore of still another island they found a stand of sea stacks, weird towers of rock sculpted by sand and wind and engulfed in flocks of gulls and cormorants, and as they banked for another look, Kate saw three bald eagles take wing. Hot springs steamed up from cupped valleys, the tall Aleutian rye grass clustering thick and still green around them.

Kate had a nagging feeling something was wrong, and took a moment to identify it. "No trees!"

"What?"

"There aren't any trees!"

Jack looked over at her with a raised eyebrow. "Even I know there aren't any trees in the Aleutians, Kate. And even I know why. The wind blows too hard."

"I know, I know, I just—I'd forgotten."

"There are trees in Unalaska, though." He nodded at her look of incredulity. "But they were brought there. I was talking to a guy yesterday. There's a stand of firs, planted by the Russians almost two hundred years ago. And it appears they are just now beginning to reproduce."

He looked at her, waiting, and she said approvingly, "Very good. Jack. Where'd you stumble across all this local color?"

"Wasn't a hell of a lot to do in Dutch Harbor, waiting for your boat to come in. I'd been sleeping in the back"—he jerked a thumb toward the back of the plane—"and she was parked off to one side of the strip, and you know how people who work around planes are. I shot the breeze with whoever felt like talking. Interesting place. Dutch, not the airstrip."

"I haven't had a chance to sightsee myself, yet. Maybe next time in, if we have any time on shore."

"With any luck, we'll find out what happened to those two yo-yos and you won't have to go out again." He peered through the windshield, squinting against the sun, and consulted a map unfolded on his lap. "That should be Anua, dead ahead."

Kate craned her neck for her first look at the little island. It had two mountains, one three thousand feet high and smoking, the other half its height and serene beneath a layer of snow. Between the two lay a valley, its surface barely above sea level, narrow and as flat as an ironing board. "I can see why they put a base here during the war," Kate observed.

"It's a natural site," Jack agreed, "and the island is right on the air route between Dutch and Adak. Good place for an emergency landing. Look, over there, south side of the island, west side of the beach. Yeah. That's where Gault says the two guys went ashore." He put the plane into a steep dive and they flew up and then down the long, curving beach.

"There's the strip," Kate said, pointing inland.

"So it is, and it looks in fair shape, too." All the same, Jack flew down the runway three times, gear five feet off the deck, checking for rocks and bumps and holes. When he was satisfied he circled again, lowered the flaps and sideslipped down to a perfect three-point landing.

Kate hid a smile and said mildly, "Show-off." If possible, Jack's expression became even more smug, and she added, "Too bad you can't do that at Merrill Field in Anchorage."

He laughed. "Too many people there. I can only do it right when nobody's watching." He cut the engine and in the sudden silence added, "This strip's in good shape. Not much snow, but what there is, is packed down. No big ruts, either. Curious. For an abandoned strip."

"Maybe hunters use it."

He shook his head. "Fishermen, maybe. Island's too small to support anything worth packing out."

The Cessna had rolled out to a stop twenty feet from a tumbledown assortment of shacks, most of them minus their roof and some missing a wall or two. Kicking through the debris, they found nothing of interest beyond a tattered, water-soaked cover of *Life* magazine featuring Betty Grable's legs, and a half-buried metal tank with a pump handle mounted on the outside. Jack tried the pump and to their surprise it worked smoothly. A few cranks and fluid gushed out of the spout, to melt and puddle in the snow on the ground. The smell of gasoline struck sharply at their nostrils.

"Av gas," Jack said.

"How do you know?"

"It's green," he said, pointing to the puddle beneath the spout. "Aviation gas is green. Plain old gas gas, like you put in your car, is clear."

"Oh. Right." Kate stared at the widening puddle, her eyebrows drawing together.

"Besides," Jack was saying, "what else kind of gas would you expect to find right next to an airstrip? I wonder how long it's been sitting here? Twenty, thirty years, you think? Might have been here since the war." Catching sight of her puzzled expression, he said, "What?"

"I don't know," she said slowly, still staring at the puddle of green gas. "There's something about av gas I remember from when I was a kid, but..." She shook her head and smiled at him. "At two o'clock this morning I'll probably sit bolt upright in bed and shout it out."

"Not if you're in the sack with me, you won't," he told her.

"Whatever you say." She grinned at him. "Come on. Let's walk down to the beach."

It was Jack who found it, or rather fell through the roof of it. He'd been wandering behind her, through the tall rye grass poking up through the thin layer of crusted snow, enjoying the sun and the salt breeze and the sound of the surf, when the previously solid ground beneath his feet gave way and suddenly he was sliding through the turf and into an empty space beneath.

"Hey," he said. The turf engulfed his legs and started up his butt to nibble at his waist and he raised his voice. "Hey? Hey!

Hey, Kate! Kate! Help! *Help!*"

He kicked out with his legs, trying to find purchase, something to brace himself against, and immediately slid in up to his chest. His hands scrabbled around and grasped at the grass, anything to keep him from sliding even farther into what his naturally strong sense of optimism assured him was probably a bubbling pit of volcanic lava. If it came to that, he suffered from a lifelong case of acrophobia, and would have preferred a pit of lava to an empty, endless abyss.

Kate's head appeared, ending this morbid speculation, and peered down at him through the rye grass with interest. "What seems to be the problem?"

"What the hell does it look like, I'm falling into the center of the earth here! Get me out!"

She looked at him, pursing her lips, displaying less concern than he considered the situation warranted. "I wonder—" Abruptly, her head vanished again from sight.

He panicked, just a little, no more than he considered absolutely necessary. "Wait! Where the hell you going? Kate!"

"Relax," he heard her say. He waited, unrelaxed, sweating beneath his jacket and clutching at some very insubstantial stalks of grass. An overactive imagination conjured up a chasm beneath his dangling legs, a bottomless chasm into which he would fall and keep falling—

Something grabbed hold of his right foot and gave a vigorous tug. "Hey!" he yelled.

"Relax," Kate said again, laughter in her voice, which seemed now to be coming from beneath him. "It's only me. The floor's about two feet beneath you. Let go and slide on down."

He hesitated. "Are you sure?"

"Would I lie to you?"

Her voice sounded entirely too innocent to suit him, but he trusted her enough to let go of the grass, one stalk at a time. Nothing happened. He raised his arms and wriggled a little. His shoulders caught in the hole for a moment, before the edges of the hole disintegrated and he slipped through in a rain of soil and grass.

Almost at once his feet hit solid ground. Staggering, he caught his balance and found himself in a small room, square, twelve feet on a side. The walls had been dug into the surface of the island and, looking up, through the dim light coming through the hole he'd made he could see that the builders had roofed the room over in turf and let the grass do the rest.

"People have been here," Kate said positively, standing next to him.

"Well, of course people have been here, Kate, even I can tell that this is a man-made structure."

"No, I mean recently," she told him. He followed her pointing finger and saw a half-dozen cases of Van Camp's Pork and Beans stacked next to a virtual tower of Costco's twenty-four-roll packages of ScotTissue Premium two-ply Bathroom Tissue.

He walked over to take a closer look. "All the essentials of life." He raised his head and stared around. "The Coasties never said anything about this place. I don't remember reading about it in any of the reports on the search missions. They must have missed it completely."

"I don't know how," Kate said, "all you have to do is fall through the roof."

Jack ignored her. "Alcala and Brown must have missed it, too. Too bad. They could have holed up here for days." One of the boxes was open, and grinning a little, he pulled out a can and held it up. "Dinner might have gotten a little monotonous, but hell." The can slipped and he almost dropped it. Something cool and gooey ran over his fingers. "What the hell?"

Even with the new skylight in the roof there wasn't enough light in the little room to see what he was talking about. "What's wrong?" she said, peering into the dim corner in which he was standing.

A booted foot crunched on sand, and she recoiled when a disembodied hand thrust a can of pork and beans in her face. "Yuk," she said, wrinkling her nose at the smell. "Somebody leave the rest of his supper behind?"

"I don't think so." Brushing by her, Jack stooped to go through the door. His voice was grim, and Kate followed him outside.

The light confirmed what his fingertips had felt. The can was punctured, a hole the size of a .38 caliber bullet entering under the V in Van and exiting just above the bottom seam.

Jack regarded the hole meditatively. "Think whoever put this stuff here used it for target practice?"

Without answering, Kate ducked back inside the dugout. Together they hauled out everything inside. As they removed each box, Jack marked it with his omnipresent black Marksalot, and they re-stacked them outside in the same position they had been in inside. The contents of the perforated cans had spilled out over the cases and dried to a sticky dark brown that looked like old blood. "Some of it might be old blood," Jack observed. The outward facing surface common to three of the boxes, the three messiest ones, looked crumpled, as if a heavy weight had slammed into them where they were stacked against the dugout's wall.

Jack stood looking at the cardboard boxes, hands in his pockets. "What we got here is two choices," he said at last.

"And they are?"

"Either somebody was really and I mean *really* tired of pork and beans."

"Or?" Their eyes met. Her mouth compressed into a thin line. "You got a can opener in the plane?"

They opened every case and then every can with a hole in it. They found a dozen such cans and, rattling around in the sixth box they opened, one lone slug. Jack held up the misshapen piece of metal and said, "This could be anything from a .22 to a .357." Nevertheless, he stored it carefully away in a Ziploc bag. Into another Ziploc he scraped some of the dried brown fluid from the front of one of the boxes. He'd brought a flashlight back with the can opener and they examined the floor of the dugout, without result. Jack bagged some samples of the dirt anyway. He made several drawings of the scene, and when he was through they repacked the cans in their cases and loaded them into the back of the Cessna. The toilet paper, which had survived the armed assault relatively unscathed—"Naturally," Jack said, "the slug would have been in a lot better shape if it had impacted the asswipe"—was stacked back where they'd found it.

The little room, dark and dank and smelling of mildew, had begun to close in around Kate and she was glad to leave it. The air outside felt fresh and clean and she pulled it into her lungs in big, cleansing breaths.

The dugout stood on the south slope of a tiny rise that fell away to the beach. Jack stood with his back to the water, looking at the structure, impressed by its air of having grown there. The rye grass grew tall and thick and right up to the walls and over the roof, and even now, in winter, from three, even two steps away, the door was invisible. He could see how the Coasties had missed it. Of course, they hadn't been looking with murder in mind. "Who built this place? And why?"

"You said this island has a natural strategic location," Kate reminded him, pulling the door closed, noting as she did that it was made of meticulously assembled planks in which no nail had been placed without careful thought and attention. "You think the Aleuts wouldn't have noticed that, too?"

He was skeptical. "You think there was a village here at one time? You think this place has been here that long?"

"Why not? It's built in the old way. Those dirt walls have been there so long they feel like concrete. Look at this door. Those planks are salvage, and old salvage at that. See? Hand-planed. And these nails? Those weren't mass-produced. Some whaler broke up offshore a hundred years ago and whoever lived here made doors out of the wreck. And that hole you fell through."

"What about it?"

"Before the Russians introduced doors, the Aleuts built these *barabaras* with the doors in the roof." She looked around. "I bet if we looked, we'd find the ruins of others."

"There are no records of a village on Anua, Kate. There's no mark on the map for archaeological ruins. This is probably just some seal hunter's cabin."

She shook her head. "The beach is long, wide and relatively level. There aren't that many good beaches in the Aleutians. Mostly it's just one steep slide from mountaintop to ocean bottom. That makes this a natural site"—she gave him a brief smile—"for landing kayaks."

They walked the ten feet to where the rye grass left off and the beach began. Over a mile in length, Kate estimated, with a jumbled rock formation on one end and cliffs on the other. A creek burbled seaward, cutting a shallow bed through the center of the beach down to the waterline. There, the surf pounded viciously at the gravel, and the ebb and flow of the swells coming in from the southeast alternately revealed and swallowed up a half-dozen reefs within the curve of the land, staggered one after the other, jagged and threatening. "Yeah," Jack said dryly, "real inviting place to beach a boat."

"They would have found a way in," Kate said, positive. "And it would have been a tremendous natural defense against attack."

"What are you looking at?"

Her eyes were squinted against the sun. "Right there, I— yes! I think it is!" she cried, pointing, and took off running.

"Oh, Christ," Jack said, and took off after her.

He caught up with her where the towers of rock broke the furious surf into white sheets of spray some hundred feet away. Not near far enough away, in his humble opinion, and he was about to say so when he saw that she was stripping out of her clothes. His heartbeat, which had started to slow down at no sign of a mad marksman with a mad on for Van Camp's Pork and Beans, began once again to speed up. "What in the hell are you doing, Shugak?"

"Look," she said, pointing in front of them.

"What?" He cast about wildly for some reason for Kate to be stripping down to the buff, on an Aleutian Island, between the Gulf of Alaska and the Bering Sea, in the middle of October.

They were standing at the edge of a tumble of rock that stretched between beach and the rock towers. The surf pounded at the towers in what Jack considered to be determined and ominous fashion. Some amphibious mammal, probably one with very large and very sharp teeth, was barking in large numbers somewhere beyond those rock towers. Gulls screamed and dived in the blue sky above. Kate gave an exasperated sigh at his confused expression and pointed again. "Right in front of you, idiot."

His gaze dropped. Directly in front of the toes of his boots, on the tumble of rock between them and the ominous surf, there was a series of shallow pools in the dips and hollows between the rocks. One of the larger pools began at their feet, stretched out some twelve feet across and looked to be some three to four feet deep. He gave the still, green surface a suspicious look. "Tidal pools?" he said. "So what?"

"Not tidal pools, hot springs!" Kate said impatiently. "See the steam! Can't you smell the sulfur?" She shucked out of panties and bra and waded in. "I knew it!" she said, feeling her way with her feet. "The bottom is almost smooth and— yes," she said, bending over and feeling beneath the surface with her hands, "I can feel where they leveled out a place to sit." She turned and lowered herself into the water. It came up almost to her chin, and she let loose with a long, voluptuous sigh. "Not too hot, not too cold, just exactly, perfectly right."

Her spirits rose with her body temperature, and the ghosts she had felt pressing about her as she worked in the dugout dissolved in the wisps of steam that rose from the water's surface. She looked at Jack, one corner of her mouth curling. The challenge was implicit. He gritted his teeth and bent over to unlace his boots. She watched with enjoyment, and went so far as to hum the tune to "The Stripper" when he got to his belt. He had a terrible time with the buttons on his jeans.

When he lowered himself into the water next to her Jack was amazed to discover that this wasn't some perfidious Shugak practical joke after all. The water was hot, but not too hot. It bubbled up around him in a natural Jacuzzi and sizzled right through his skin into his bones. "Oh, yeah," he said, relaxing with a long, satisfied groan. Curious, he tasted the water. "It's not very salty," he said in surprise.

"It's probably a mixture," she said, leaning back and closing her eyes. "Salt from the spray, fresh from underground."

He looked over and admired the way her body shone up at him through the water. It was a perfect body in his eyes, compact, well muscled, just the right balance of lean to soft, lithe in motion and at rest. Her face was broad across the cheekbones, softening to a small, stubborn chin that held up a wide, determined mouth. Her hazel eyes tilted up at the sides with the hint of an epicanthic fold. Even the twisted scar that stretched across her throat almost from ear to ear looked right today, a badge of honor, an emblem of courage. A warning, too. Anyone who had a scar like that and was still around to wear it was not someone you wanted to mess with.

She opened her eyes and caught him admiring, and after that they didn't talk for a while.

"Nice day," Jack said, in an inadequate expression of postcoital bliss.

"Enjoy it." Kate replied, her face nuzzled into his neck. "It'll get worse."

The lover in him didn't move a muscle. The pilot looked nervously over her head to the southeast for signs of an incoming weather front, and found only the merest wisps of cloud low on the horizon. "How do you know?"

"Because in the Aleutians the one rule is, if the weather is good, it'll get bad. And if it's bad, it'll get worse. During the war, the air force lost two times the amount of casualties and five times the amount of planes to weather and mechanical trouble due to weather than they did in combat." She mustered up enough energy to point. "See the end of the runway?"

He didn't bother to turn his head. "Sure."

"You're lucky. It was more than the World War II pilots

could see. They didn't have radar at first and the weather'd be so bad the pilot waiting for takeoff would have to radio to the guy taking off in front of him to find out if he'd left the ground or not, before he could make his try." She raised her head and looked at him. "And then, once they were in the air, assuming of course they did make it into the air, they were flying on naval charts based on a Russian survey made in 1864. Assuming of course they could see anything once they got into the air."

"Sounds like fun to me." He rubbed the small of her back, surveying the treeless expanse of bog and rock, and the heaving, swelling sea stretching endlessly beyond. "Why'd they bother?"

"They had to. If the Japanese took Alaska, they'd have been within bombing range of Boeing. Not to mention Russia. There's only fifty-seven miles of water between the Alaskan and Russian coasts. It was a major Lend-Lease route, through Fairbanks and Nome." She added, "Plus, the Japanese lost at Midway because they were attacking Dutch Harbor at the same time. It split their forces at a time when they were infinitely superior to us in the Pacific."

"Divide and conquer."

"Something like that."

"You know a lot about it."

"There's a book, a good one, on the war in the Aleutians, written by a guy named Garfield. And..."

"And what?"

"And," Kate said, a little embarrassed to discover she was proud of it, "my uncle was one of Castner's Cutthroats."

Jack looked blank. "One of what?"

"Castner's Cutthroats. Also known as the Alaska Scouts." He drew back and looked down at her questioningly.

"Don't stop there. Were they some sort of troops, or what?"

Kate grinned. "More 'or what,' if you could believe my uncle. They were kind of like Special Forces, long on fighting ability and short on discipline, but you could expect that from the kind of men they were. Castner must have hit every bar in the bush signing them up. Old Sam said there were prospectors, homesteaders, doctors, hunters, trappers, fishermen. I think they even bagged an anthropologist or two, probably out of the University of Alaska."

"They see any action?"

"They went ashore at Attu before the regular troops. It was in-your-face fighting every step of the way. There was even a banzai charge with bayonets, near the end, when the Japanese knew they were beat." Kate shivered. "Messy. Oh, yeah, Old Sam could strip his sleeves and show his scars with the best of them."

"Shock troops."

"I guess." Kate looked around again. "I wonder what happened to them."

"Who, Castner's Cutthroats?"

"No. The Anuans."

The rock seat beneath him having been worn indisputably smooth by generations of buttocks before he had taken up residence, Jack was no longer disposed to argue over the existence of an Aleut settlement on Anua. "Maybe they were moved out during the war."

"You said there was no record of a settlement on Anua," she reminded him.

"Oh, yeah. Right." He thought. "Didn't I just read something in the papers about how Congress passed an act to compensate the Aleutian Aleuts for being uprooted from their homes during World War II?"

Kate nodded. "Yeah. In 1989. The survivors got sixteen bucks for every day they spent in the camps."

"What did happen, back then? I never have heard the full story."

Kate's shoulders moved in a faint shrug. "It was war, the Japanese had attacked Pearl Harbor and invaded Attu and Kiska. The military authorities could pretty much do as they liked, so they bundled up every last Aleut from the Rat Islands north and settled them in villages in southcentral Alaska. After the war, almost none of them were resettled in their original villages, and the soldiers trashed what little housing was left standing. They'd burned or bulldozed most of it anyway, either to keep the Japs from using it or to make way for their own construction."

"But it was war," Jack pointed out.

"I know."

"If things had gone the other way, they could have wound up prisoners of the Japanese."

"Some of them did. Some Aleuts the Japanese took prisoner off Attu and Kiska. In Japan, they put them to work, and even paid them for it." Kate smiled. "When they were repatriated, their biggest difficulty was in getting their Japanese paychecks cashed."

"How come you know so much about this?"

A muscle cramped in her thigh and she grunted and shifted off him. He whimpered a little in protest but didn't stop her. "Jack, I'm an Aleut." She waited for that to register, but he looked blank. "I'm an Aleut living in an area historically inhabited by Athapascans, Eyaks and Tlingits." His blank expression began to change to comprehension, and she nodded. "My family comes from around here somewhere. We were expatriated along with the rest of the Aleuts. We had relatives in Cordova, so we moved to the Park."

"No wonder you took this job."

She ducked her head, embarrassed again, this time to be discovered in a moment of racial sentimentality. "Yeah. I guess I just wanted to see what the old home place looked like." She squinted up at the sun and added, "We'd better get a move on if we want to make it back to Dutch before dark."

"I've got a tarp in the back of the plane," he said, reaching for his pants.

"So?"

"So, we can tack it over that hole I made in the roof of the dugout."

"*Barabara.*"

"Whatever."

Her smile was reward enough for the thought, and realizing it, he knew he had it bad. In the air the following morning, when he banked the Cessna for a last look at the honeymoon suite in the hot springs, he was sure of it.

As they climbed another thousand feet, over the sound of the engine Kate said, "You think somebody got shot in the *barabara!*"

"Yup."

"Maybe somebody who was hiding out from somebody else?"

"Yup."

Kate was unable to keep herself from wondering which one. Alcala or Brown. The sexy ascetic or the teddy bear. Whose dried and darkened blood had it been that had spilled over the cardboard cases, had mingled with the gravy oozing from the broken cans and dripped down, to lose all color and identity until it became one with the dirt floor?

Could have been both, she realized. No reason why not.

The mental picture of the two young men, spending the remaining minutes of their lives cowering between the cases of pork and beans and the rolls of toilet paper, was enough to keep her silent all the way back to Dutch.

CHAPTER 4

KATE OPENED THE DOOR into her stateroom and found a human pretzel in the middle of the floor. The pretzel shifted and there was a flash of bleached blond hair. "Andy? Is that you?" All the relaxed sense of well-being acquired over the last twenty-four hours abandoned her in a rush and she jumped forward, the heavy wooden door banging shut behind her.

"What?" In a single, sinuous twist, the human pretzel resolved itself into a long, lanky human with blond hair flopping into his thin, earnest face. "What's wrong, Kate?"

Kate stared at him, her mouth open. "For a minute I thought—what the hell was that?"

Andy dropped forward, his forehead on his knees, his body folded forward like a cherry popover. "What was what?"

"What you were doing!" she roared, her voice a furious husk of sound. "What *are* you doing?"

He popped erect, looking bewildered. "It's only yoga, Kate."

"Yoga! Yoga?"

"Sure. You want me to teach you?"

"Yoga." She pulled herself together. "I don't think so. I am not partial to twisting myself into anything it doesn't look like I could twist myself back out of unassisted."

He rippled to his feet and ran an impersonal finger over her shoulder. "You're strong and fairly supple." He poked her deltoid muscle with a critical frown. "Probably wouldn't be hard to get down a few of the more basic moves."

"No," Kate said, stepping out of range, "I don't think so. Thank you all the same."

Andy, sure that she was only waiting to be convinced, insisted, "Hatha yoga is the yoga of physical well-being. It helps you find harmony, and peace of mind, and true happiness. You'll sleep better and sounder, your tensions will diminish—"

"The tension alone I get from rooming with you, nothing could diminish."

"Plus your disposition will improve," he observed.

Kate took a deep breath and managed a smile. "My disposition doesn't need improving, thank you."

He shook his head disapprovingly. "You're so resistant, Kate. I'm going to have to do something about that."

What scared her most was that he might succeed.

• • •

They left Dutch Harbor on the evening tide and were pulling pots in the Gulf of Alaska thirty-six hours later. The halogen lights mounted on the cabin illuminated the *Avilda*'s deck and nothing else; the fog was back with a vengeance, as if in retaliation for the one perfect day. The swells, too, were increasing, long, slow swells that came in from the southeast, each one higher than the last, making Ned Nordhoff shake his head and mutter into his beard. He climbed the ladder to the bridge and Kate saw him arguing vociferously with Harry Gault. A few minutes later he was back on deck, his face red beneath his beard and his voice curt.

The first pot they pulled had half a dozen Dungeness and a pollock inside it. "Garbage," Ned growled, and hoisted the

71

pot over to Andy and Kate. They opened the door, tossed the dungies and the gasping bottomfish over the side, re-baited the pot and tied the door shut again. Something about the pot bothered Kate but by then the next pot was aboard and routine took over.

The second pot came in, as empty as the first one of anything harvestable, and gloom settled in on deck. A crew share of nothing was nothing. Still they went through the motions, pulling, baiting and resetting. Kate wondered why the skipper didn't tell them to stack the pots on deck, to set them somewhere else, because the tanner had obviously vacated this part of the ocean for greener sea bottoms elsewhere.

It wasn't until the sixth pot in the string that the nagging feeling clicked over to recognition. "Hey," she said, puzzled. She looked at the yellow ties holding the door of the pot closed. "Andy, you're a southpaw, aren't you?"

"Yeah."

"So your wrap on the door ties would go this way. Right?"

He stared for a moment. "I guess so."

"Show me. Tie one."

He reached for the twine, his fingers moving slowly and clumsily, making several false starts. "It's harder to do when you're thinking about it," he apologized. Finished, he stepped back.

"Uh-huh," Kate said. "See? Your hitches go the other way around. You didn't tie these," she elaborated when he looked mystified. "And look at the bait jar."

"What about it?"

"I use a becket to hang our jars. That looks like some kind of granny knot." She raised her voice. "Hey, Ned? Come here a minute, would you?"

There was a responding growl next to the pot launcher and Ned materialized out of the fog, which had thickened into a gray-green soup that swirled and eddied all around them. "What?" he asked sarcastically. "The kid making suggestive remarks about your ass?"

"What can he say except that it's perfect?" she snapped back. "Look at this."

"Look at what? I don't see anything."

Kate, holding on to her temper, said evenly, "Somebody's been at these pots before us." She showed him the ties and the bait jar.

"The shots are coming up tangled, too," Seth said from behind Ned, "and the bridles don't look right, either."

Ned examined the knots, and they waited. An oath ripped out that singed the ears of his listeners and he turned to make for the bridge ladder. After a moment the *Avilda*'s engine settled into a low, neutral purr and Ned returned to the deck with the skipper at his heels.

Gault's mouth worked soundlessly and his face slowly reddened as he looked at the door ties and the bait jar. The rest of the crew waited, Seth impassive, Andy nervous, Kate watchful.

Ned said something to Gault and was waved away with an abrupt movement. "It's that fucking Johansen on the fucking *Daisy Mae* again," the skipper spat. "This time I don't take it lying down." His grin was mirthless and malevolent when he added, "This time I know where the little prick's pots are."

"It's not worth it," Seth said, his voice as clear as it was unexpected. "We shouldn't take chances, not with what else we've got going—" He looked over at the rest of the crew, hesitated and said, "It's not worth the grief we'll get from the owners if they ever find out about it."

73

"I don't give a damn what they say in Freetown!" Gault yelled. "I don't grab my ankles every time Freetown says bend over! Secure the deck and rig for running!"

Gault returned to the bridge. Ned and Seth exchanged a long glance. Seth shrugged, and Ned growled, "You heard the man. Secure the deck."

Andy looked bewildered. "What do we do with the pot? We need to dump out the garbage and bait it, right?"

"You got a hearing problem, Blondie?" the deck boss demanded. "The skipper said dump it."

"But what about the rest of the string?"

"Dump it!"

They dumped it, the bait jar empty, the pot still holding three immature tanners, the fragile pink of their shells testifying to a recent molt. Almost before the water closed over the bridle, the *Avilda* was coming about in a 180-degree turn, and if the whining protest of the engine was any indication, the throttle was open all the way. Kate stood at the railing, face into the wind, and breathed deep of the salt air.

"Somebody robbed our pots, is that it?" Andy said, coming up behind her.

"That's it," she agreed.

"Somebody pulled them and picked the legal tanners and left the junk—the garbage," he corrected himself, "for us."

"Looks that way."

"Who would do that?" he said, his voice shocked. "Who would steal from their fellow fishermen like that?"

Kate, amused and a trifle touched by his innocence, said, "Probably somebody on their way out to their own string stumbled across ours and got a little greedy. Although it sounds like the skipper knows exactly who did it, which means it's happened before."

"So what's going on?" Andy asked her. "What're we doing now? Are we going back to Dutch? Are we calling the cops?"

"I don't know," she said, although she had a pretty good idea. When the Anchorage District Attorney's accounting department found bail money listed as an expense incurred in the investigation of this case, Kate hoped they found it in their hearts to pass it through.

The *Avilda* ran flat out and north-northeast, in six hours fetching up just south of the Islands of Four Mountains. There, they ran back and forth, quartering and subdividing the seas off Yunaska. The fog had thickened and Kate was glad, but then a buoy slid by the port rail, and she resigned herself. There just wasn't going to be any getting out of this one.

Seth, moving more quickly than Kate had ever seen him move before, had a boat hook over the side and hooked on to the buoy before it passed out of reach. When it proved to be a buoy belonging to the *Daisy Mae*, the deck crew could hear Harry's shriek of triumph right through the walls of the bridge.

When Seth pinched a section of the rope and started the winch to pull the pot, Kate knew enough to keep her mouth shut. Andy didn't.

"Wait a minute," he said, "those aren't our buoys." When Ned ignored him, he caught his arm. "Hey, Ned. I said we aren't picking our own pots."

"I heard you," Ned grunted, shaking him off. "Sort that goddam crab, Blondie."

Andy stared from Ned to Seth, and lastly to Kate, who was coiling the incoming line into a wet pile at her feet. He opened his mouth to say more. She gave her head a small, single shake. Her steady gaze held a clear, silent warning, and Andy, if naive, was not stupid. He shut his mouth and stepped forward to help pull the pot on board.

It was only the beginning. For five hours they picked pots that weren't theirs. On the bridge Gault worked the spotlight, picking the next set of buoys out of the fog, while he watched the radar for approaching vessels. On deck, with a grin of pure enjoyment on his face and a knife in his hand, Ned slashed through the pot webbing. His face expressionless, Seth cut bait jars loose and pitched them over the side, and then cut the shots of line, once where it attached to the bridle of each pot and again below the buoys. They were good solid pots, one-and-a-quarter-inch mild steel, with zinc anodes to retard rusting. When the pot did go overboard, it was a seven-by-seven-by-three-foot 750-pound piece of junk. Even if it could be salvaged, it would have to almost entirely be remade before it was fishable again.

Kate, working silently and efficiently alongside the rest of the crew, was sickened, both at the display of spite and at the waste of equipment. She worried about Andy, who worked next to her mechanically, a strained look on his pale face. "You okay?" she asked him in a low voice. He nodded without replying and she had to be satisfied with that.

They pulled pots, they sorted crab, they slashed webbing, they cut line, they punctured buoys, until their backs ached and their heads hurt. They hurried for fear of discovery, and spoke only seldom, and then in whispers. What made it worse was that Johansen wasn't on the crab at all and the pots coming up were mostly garbage. One had what Kate would have sworn was at least a thousand pounds of females in it, another only a couple of chicken halibut. If she'd known how hard thieving was, and how unrewarding, she might have made more of a protest in the beginning.

Straightening her back and groaning a little, she noticed that the sound of the *Avilda*'s, engine had changed. A loud whisper floated down from the catwalk in front of the bridge, and she looked up to see Harry Gault motioning to her.

"Got a boat coming up on us on the screen," he said in a hoarse whisper. "Tell Ned we're taking off."

They stripped the deck bare of any shred of the *Daisy Mae*'s gear, pitching it all over the side. In his haste Andy pitched over a couple of their own knives and a twenty-five-fathom shot of their own line, too. He gave Ned a fearful look.

Ned was feeling very pleased with life, and shrugged in response to Andy's look. "No problem. Plenty more where they came from."

The rumble of the diesel increased and Kate sent up a fervent hope that the old girl's engine held together long enough for a clean getaway. Sound carried over water, and the other boat undoubtedly had its own radar. They had to know the *Avilda* was there, and if the pots belonged to them, they had to know what the *Avilda* had been up to. Kate just hoped they didn't have a rifle.

Their luck held. The *Avilda* was unpursued. They ran flat-out for eight hours through the fog to the beginning of their own string. There followed a grueling twenty-four hours with no stops of pulling pots, re-baiting and resetting them. Toward the end of the string the pots suddenly began coming up loaded, which meant they had worked their way beyond where the pot robbers had stopped or been scared off by the approach of another boat. More crab went in the hold and the atmosphere on deck improved. This trip out the weather was infinitely better, fog or no fog, and the crew worked much more swiftly and efficiently. Although Kate did miss the big swells when it came to shoving pots that outweighed her by 630 pounds across a deck that seemed to have increased considerably in width between this trip and the last.

They were clearing the deck and covering the hold when a hammering on the bridge window made the deck crew look up. Harry was circling his extended forefinger in the air. He went so far as to open a window and yell, "I'll bring 'er in, the rest of you get some shut-eye."

As before when the skipper had given the signal for home, Ned trotted astern and tossed a short length of one-inch manila line overboard, its bound end looped around a cleat on the stern rail, its free end trailing behind, twisting and turning in the wake of white foam.

Andy watched covertly from amidships, and nudged Kate when Ned passed forward. "What's that line for?" he asked in a low voice. "It's not connected to anything, it's just dragging behind us."

Kate was standing at the railing, her face into the wind, as if the cold, clear sea air could scour her clean of the taint of the night's activities. Following his gaze, tired as she was, she smiled and replied in the same low voice, "It's the lady's line."

"The what?"

She opened the door into the galley. "The lady's line. It's an old sailors' custom, dates back before the whalers, I think."

"What does it mean?" he said, following her down the passageway.

"When it comes time to turn for home, they toss a free line in the water, so the ladies they left behind can pull their loved ones home."

Andy thought it over, his face brightening a little. "I like it. It's got tradition."

"Don't say anything about it," Kate told him, still in a low voice. "It's not talked about, it's just done."

He grinned a tired grin. "Don't want to break the spell, huh?"

"Do you walk under ladders?"

His grin faded and he paused, the door to their room halfway open. "Do you let black cats cross your path?" Kate asked him. "When you spill salt, do you quick toss a pinch of it over your shoulder? Do you knock wood when you say something that might tempt fate?" He didn't answer, of course, and she smiled again, following him into their room. "Don't say anything about the lady's line. Nobody likes having their superstitions made fun of."

"I don't care what they do on the *Avilda* anyway," he said, his momentary animation passing off, leaving his face white and weary. "I'm getting off this boat, Kate. Anybody who could do that to somebody else's livelihood... how much does a seven-by cost?"

"I don't know. Three, four hundred, something like that."

"And all that polypro, and the buoys, and the bait jars. Not to mention the time lost fishing." He closed his eyes and repeated firmly, "I don't know where I'm going, but I'm getting off this boat."

She put a comforting hand on his shoulder. "That's life in the big leagues, Andy."

"It's not my life," he declared. "And I bet I can find me a skipper who feels the same way. When I do, I'm outta here." Without another word he stripped down to his longies and climbed into his bunk. The snores that almost immediately issued from the top bunk made Kate wish for as clear a conscience.

So completely had she been immersed in the role of able-bodied seaman cum apprentice pot pirate that she was halfway out of her own clothes when she remembered why she had signed on the *Avilda* in the first place. Simultaneously she realized that with the rest of the crew in the sack and the skipper on watch, now was the perfect time to toss Harry Gault's stateroom.

Andy didn't skip a snore when she cracked the door and slipped into the passageway. The snores coming from behind Ned and Seth's door were so loud she wondered how either of them could sleep. At least she didn't have to sneak. She wasn't up to it.

The skipper's cabin was the one closest to the galley. True, it was only a step from his door to the stairs leading up to the bridge, but Kate disapproved. The truly conscientious skipper, in her experience, slept in the chart room bunk at sea so as to be close to the bridge, not the galley. Still, it made it easier for her to break and enter, and she was grateful for that if for nothing else.

Not that there was much breaking to the entering. The door to his cabin was unlocked and swung smoothly and noiselessly inward, closing with a silent click behind her. She flicked on the light.

It was the same stateroom repeated twice on each side of the passageway, a small square room with over and under bunk beds built into the bulkhead. A single porthole was set between the bunks, drawers beneath the bottom one. What wasn't standard issue was an old steel desk that had army surplus written all over it jammed in next to the beds, and a two-drawer filing cabinet next to it, same lineage.

After one look Kate didn't want to step foot inside the tiny bathroom opening off one side of the room for fear of catching something, what she didn't know, but something unpleasant was definitely growing in the saucer-sized sink. She didn't bother looking in the shower, mostly because she was afraid of what she'd find. The drawers beneath the bottom bunk were the dirty clothes hamper and from the smell had been so since sometime last year. She closed the second drawer hastily without bothering to paw through the contents.

With deep reluctance she turned to the desk. If there was one thing Kate hated more than flying in anything bigger than a Cessna 172, it was paperwork.

At first all she found were fish tickets and delivery statements. As a matter of curiosity she rummaged until she found the ticket from their last run, and was annoyed but unsurprised to find that Harry Gault had shorted the crew on their shares of the last delivery.

The engine beat steadily up through the floor. Yawning, she left the desk for the file cabinet. It was locked, but a few moments with a straightened paper clip had the top drawer open. Each drawer was stuffed with paper, but stuffed in an orderly and alphabetical way that belied the confusion of the desk. Jack Morgan could have learned something from Harry Gault's filing system. She pulled a file and thumbed through it, yawning again and hoping she wasn't going to nod off. Hairy Gault coming in off watch to find her dozing at his desk might be more than even Kate could explain away.

The first file she pulled was a collection of lease-purchase agreements between a Henderson Gantry of Ketchikan, Alaska, and various sellers of boats. From the physical description of each boat, most of them appeared to be service boats, tenders that ran between fishing grounds and canneries, or between oil rigs and town carrying supplies and crew changes, or ran pilots out to incoming very large crude carriers on their way in and out of Valdez. Kate thought it looked like the beginning of a fair-sized fleet. All of the agreements were dated in April and May of 1989, and all of them were underwritten by the same bank, in Ketchikan, Alaska. Interesting. A fair-sized fleet all bought at the same time and through not only the same bank but the same loan officer.

Henderson Gantry. Harry Gault. If they were one and the same, what was Harry doing with all these boats? "I thought you were strictly a hired hand, Harry old buddy," she murmured. She opened another file, and raised her eyebrows.

A fair-sized fleet that evidently was not making enough money to meet its mortgage payments. This file held warning notices from a bank. Not *a* bank, she noticed, but half a dozen different banks, and none of them Alaskan. She went back to the first file, puzzled. Yes, the Southeast First Bank had financed the purchase of the little fleet—her eyes widened, and she set the second file down on the desk next to the first and searched farther in the file cabinet. She found what she was looking for in short order.

Almost immediately upon final signing of the original mortgages, all of the boats had been refinanced through other banks, Outside banks, most of them located in the Pacific Northwest, although two were refinanced through two different banks in San Francisco. This time the boats' owner was listed as a Harley Gruber, with impeccable references and a credit rating that would have made the city of Cleveland gnash its teeth in envy.

Kate made notes of names, dates, boats and banks, lips pursed around a soundless whistle. Harley Gruber, Henderson Gantry, Harry Gault. In her experience, people who assumed aliases almost always used names beginning with the same initials. "What have you been up to, Harry old buddy," she said under her breath, "that you need a new name every time you change business partners?"

She reached for another file and discovered one possible answer.

The latest file held lease agreements with Royal Petroleum Company. Each of the boats purchased in the Southeast had been leased to RPetCo for use in the cleanup of the *RPetCo Anchorage,* which had run aground off Bligh Reef in March of 1989 and spilled over ten million gallons of North Slope crude oil across the western half of Prince William Sound. The spill had virtually canceled the salmon fishing season that year, wiped out shrimp beds and entire schools of spawning herring, annihilated ducks and geese and terns and murres by the thousands, killed sea otters—in short, with a large and malicious sense of indiscrimination, the spill had spread a path of death and destruction across eight hundred miles of previously pristine wildlife habitat and Alaskan coastline.

If Kate lived in the Park, Prince William Sound was her backyard. She had relatives in Cordova and Tatitlek and Valdez and Seldovia and Kodiak and Iliamna who were still hurting from the spill, spiritually and financially, to this day, four years later. If Harry Gault or Henderson Gantry or Harley Gruber or whoever the hell he was had had anything to do with the farce of a cleanup that followed that devastating spill and its many peculiar financial arrangements with a relatively few, select boat owners, she, Ekaterina Ivana Shugak, would personally have Harry Gault's or Henderson Gantry's or Harley Gruber's balls served up on a platter for Sunday brunch. Wide awake now, she went to work with a vengeance.

As she was finishing up her notes and preparing a second assault on the filing cabinet, there was a thump overhead. There were no other sounds, nothing to indicate that Harry was doing anything but checking the chart, but Kate decided she had pressed her luck far enough. And she had enough to go on with. More than enough. She grinned, thinking of Jack's expression when he heard her story and saw her notes. The grin faded a little when she remembered Alcala and Brown, and she gave the files a speculative look. Was this information important enough for Harry Gault to kill two men for? She tried to remember, if she had ever known, the penalties for fraud and embezzlement. Her area of expertise had always been assault and murder; white-collar crime was out of her league. She yawned again, and wondered if collusion in the matter of who got the plum jobs on the spill cleanup could be prosecuted under the RICO statutes.

An involuntary chuckle rippled out of her torn throat. She was getting sleepy again, and silly with it, and it wasn't her problem anyway. Jack Morgan wanted background on Harry Gault, and background on Harry Gault he would get. Working quickly but not carelessly, she reassembled the documents into their original files and the files into the cabinet. A few more seconds work with the paper clip and it was locked again. Pocketing her notes and cracking the door, she eyed the empty passageway for a moment before slipping outside and pulling the door shut soundlessly behind her.

She turned and bumped straight into Harry Gault. "Oof."

With great restraint she managed to keep herself from bolting down the passageway in a panic. "Oh. Sorry, skipper. I didn't see you standing there."

His eyes flickered between her and the door to his cabin. Had he seen her come out, or had he just come down the stairs from the bridge? "What're you doing up? I thought I told Ned for everybody to get some shut-eye."

She scratched and produced a face-splitting yawn. "I woke up thirsty," she mumbled in a grumpy voice. The best defense is a good offense, and she gave him an impudent grin. "What about you? What're you doing down here? Who's steering the boat?"

"The autopilot."

"Oh." She manufactured another yawn. "Well, I'm going to get some pop. You want something?"

"No." He added grudgingly, "Thanks."

"No prob. See you in the A.M."

In the galley she stood holding on to the door handle of the refrigerator, her head pressed up against the cold enameled surface, waiting for the shaking in her knees to stop. That had been too close.

The snores from the top bunk didn't miss a beat as she stripped and slid into her own. She was so tired she ached with it, but she tossed and turned, unable to shut down her brain. Eventually she fell into a doze and a series of waking dreams, filled with ruined pots rusting on the ocean bottom and avenging fishermen coming after her with boat hooks and bank statements with overdrawn accounts and bills with red warning notices and pink crabs swimming in green gasoline. Sleep deserted her in a rush and she sat bolt upright in bed. "Pink!"

"What?" Andy's drowsy, startled voice came from the bunk overhead.

"Pink!" she said. "Old aviation gas used to be pink! Pink as a tanner's new shell, by God!"

There was a brief silence, followed by a click as Andy turned his reading light on. A tousled blond head peered over the side of the bunk. "I beg your pardon?"

"New aviation gas is green," she explained. "But the old aviation gas was pink. I remember from helping my foster father gas up his Supercub."

The befuddled expression on the upside-down face didn't

change. "And you think *I'm* weird."

The head disappeared, the light went off and Kate was left lying wide-eyed in the dark, her mind busy with this new piece of the puzzle.

CHAPTER 5

"OLD AVIATION GAS, WHAT we used to call 80/87, was pink," Kate told Jack the following afternoon over greasy hamburgers and even greasier fries at the Blow-In Cafe.

"So?"

"So the gas in that tank on Anua was green." He paused in mid-chew and looked uncomprehending. "Don't you get it? If that gas had been left over from a long time ago, it would have been pink. How long has aviation gas been green?"

Jack's face cleared and he swallowed and said, "Somebody's been using the strip regular enough to need to refuel."

Kate bestowed an approving smile on him and he sat up straighter in his chair. "And the strip was maintained, too," he remembered, "or at least there had been traffic in and out recently. Enough to keep the snow packed down, anyway. Not that there is much out here." He looked at her. "It surprised me."

"What?"

"So little snow."

"The mean winter temperature out here is thirty degrees Fahrenheit," she told him. "And I think the average snowfall is less than two feet. Plus you've got the jet stream just offshore."

Jack looked out the window at the wind blowing fog and a few flakes of snow straight down Iliuliuk Bay and shivered inwardly. "A nearly tropical climate," he agreed. "How'd you do out there, this time? Kill lots of defenseless crabs?"

"More than we should have."

"Oh, my," he said with his quick grin, "do I detect the tone of someone who has been involved in high seas skulduggery? Have you been keeping five-inchers?"

"No, just committing grand theft and malicious mischief," she replied. Her tone was glum; the imp of perverse pleasure she had taken in her first larcenous action had deserted her, and all she could think of was the crew of the *Daisy Mae* circling round and round, pulling buoys attached to nothing, not even line, and coming into Dutch with an empty hold and an emptier deck.

Jack sat up straight in his chair, hamburger dripping mustard and grease down his hand and into his sleeve. "Mind telling me what the hell that means?"

Kate told him about the pot robbing. Jack was more amused than outraged, but then Jack wasn't a fisherman. "Pretty gutsy of Gault," he observed.

"It was dumb," Kate said flatly. "There's forty thousand plus pots in the Bering Sea during any given period and hundreds of boats picking them. Not to mention the Fish and Game. It's a miracle we weren't caught. If we had been, we would have lost an entire season's fishing, and you're talking a gross anywhere between one million to two million dollars." Jack choked over his next bite of hamburger and had recourse to his Coke to wash it down. Kate, unheeding, punctuated her words with a militant french fry. "And Gault had no proof, none, that it was Johansen who robbed our string." She noticed the french fry was getting cold and crammed it into her mouth. Around it, she said indistinctly, "Dumb. If Gault hadn't married into the family, he would have been out on his ear long since."

"How long you in for this time?"

Kate shrugged. "Engine broke down again."

"That happened last week."

"I get the feeling it happened the week before and the week before that, too. Gault's not giving the engine the maintenance it needs. He's not giving the old girl any of the attention she deserves, he just drives her until she breaks, fixes it with spit and baling wire and drives her some more. One of these days she's going to break down for good. I just hope we're not out in the doughnut hole when it happens."

"'Doughnut hole'?"

Kate gestured in the general direction of the North Pacific Ocean. "Starts around the Pribilof Islands and ends, I don't know, somewhere off the Kamchatka Peninsula. Sort of an international free-for-all area for fishermen from all over."

"Beyond the two-hundred-mile limit," he suggested.

"Way beyond," Kate agreed. "The U.S. and Russia and Korea and Taiwan and Japan have been fighting in the U.N. for years for the rights to fish there. The nations have, anyway. The fishermen just fish, most of them with drift nets that drag the sea bottom and pull up everything that gets in the way. Which the biologists figure is why the crab stocks took such a dive in the mid-eighties."

Jack examined his greasy fingers with rapt attention before beginning to clean them with his napkin, slowly, meticulously, one at a time. "Listen, Kate," he said to his left ring finger, "I don't mean to sound like some nervous granny here, and I trust you to take care of yourself or I would never have set you up in this job, but—" He looked up and caught her eye, very serious. "There are survival suits on board the *Avilda*, aren't there?"

She gave him a thin smile. "First thing I checked."

"Got one for everybody?" She nodded. "They all in working order?"

She nodded again. "Unlike the *Avilda*.'"

"And life rafts?"

He knew how many life rafts there were from the reports on Alcala and Brown's disappearance, but she answered him patiently. "Two, mounted on the roof, one port, one starboard."

"Good. Not that I'm anxious about you or anything."

"Of course not," Kate agreed, still patient. The male instinct to protect was as irritating as it was infrequently endearing, but there was nothing to be done but wait until it had run its course. Probably had something to do with testosterone. There ought to be a test, like one of those early pregnancy tests, only this would be an early testosterone test to detect large buildups of testosterone in male children. They could tattoo the results on every male child's forehead; that way, unsuspecting females could tell at a glance how deep the waters were around this particular island of manly pride. She looked across the table measuringly. It was an idea whose time had come.

Jack, unsuspecting, mopped up the rest of his ketchup with his last remaining fry, regarded it sadly and swallowed it regretfully. "Nothing like a grease-soaked french fry to start your day off right," he observed. Tapping the notes she had given him, he said, "I'll call town and have someone start checking on Harley Gruber and Henderson Gantry."

"Five'll get you ten Gruber, Gantry and Gault are one and the same."

"No bet." He tried out one of his better leers. "Care to join me? I won't be on the phone that long."

"You find a room?" she said, surprised. "I can't believe the state is going to pay for any more three-hundred-dollar nights in the Shipwreck."

He hooked a thumb in the general direction of the harbor. "I talked one of the processors out of a bunk. More like a little apartment, actually. Manager's on vacation. Come with?"

"Where is it?" He told her and she rose to her feet. "I'll be down later. This might be my only chance to get to Unalaska. I'd like to see what it looks like."

• • •

Amaknak Island was connected to Unalaska Island by a five-hundred-foot bridge, the Bridge to the Other Side. Less than a mile beyond that bridge was the village of Unalaska, a town of less traffic and more village than Dutch Harbor.

Unalaska occupied a special place in Alaskan history. The Russians came there, centuries before, for the same reason the crab fishermen were there now, and the military during World War II, and that was because it had the best natural harbor in a thousand miles of Aleutian Islands. But the Aleuts had been there before them all, rich in culture and natural resources, earning a living from a bountiful if harsh marine environment, eventually sitting ducks for civilization in the form of the Russian Orthodox religion, the company store and the clap. Dragooned into slaughtering seals and sea otters almost to the point of extinction to supply the Asian fur trade, the Aleuts fought back, only to be quashed by superior firepower. The fur market collapsed, Alaska was sold to the United States and Russian traders gave way to New England whalers, the whalers to gold prospectors, the prospectors to the United States military. And now this latest invasion: fishermen and processors, American, Korean, Japanese, Russian, Taiwanese, literally scraping the bottom of the North Pacific Ocean to feed the world's insatiable appetite for seafood.

The road topped a little rise between two small hills and the rooftops of the village came into view. It wasn't much more than a string of buildings lined up along the water, enclosed by one gravel road that ran down the beach and a second that ran down the side of the truncated river that drained Unalaska Lake into Iliuliuk Bay. The buildings were a colorful jumble of frame houses, trailers and World War II-vintage cottages and cabanas, one and two stories high, some old and weathered gray by wind and salt spray, some new with the unmistakable mark of Outside prefabrication stamped firmly upon them. It reminded Kate of Niniltna, both in location and construction. She saw orange fluorescent buoys offshore, probably mooring buoys for the villagers' boats. There was an old clapboard church with two cupolas, each with onion domes surmounted by the distinctive Russian Orthodox crosses with the slanted foot bar that Christ was supposed to have twisted in his agony during the Crucifixion.

The beach was a narrow strip of gray sand, and Kate, always a sucker for beaches, walked around the end of the village, through the tall grass poking up through the crusted snow, and down to the wet sand separating sod and tide. The fog swirled overhead and offshore, and although she could hear Dutch Harbor going energetically about its business less than half a mile away across the water, the noise seemed muted. The beach stretched out before her, and she began to walk. A big New England dory loomed up out of the fog and grated against the gravel. Kate caught the bow and tugged it farther up the beach. The dory's owner hopped out and nodded his thanks. Kate walked on and the fog swallowed him up again. Farther down the beach two more figures resolved from shadow to solid shape, a father instructing his young, solemn son in the art of mending nets. The needle in his gnarled hands stilled and they looked at her without speaking until she moved on.

Wavelets from the wakes of passing boats lapped at the shore. The fog felt cool and misty on her cheeks. Because it obscured her vision, her ears worked overtime and she heard them long before she saw them. A group of girls squatted in a circle at the edge of the water, where the sand was wettest. Soft-footed, Kate came up behind them and paused to look over their shoulders.

One of the girls' legs was twisted beneath her at an awkward angle. Her body was bulky, her head too small for it. Her nose seemed to have no bridge, only nostrils, and she wheezed a little when she breathed through it. She was speaking, and at first Kate thought she must be speaking in Aleut, and then realized that the girl must have a cleft palate. She wasn't the only one who couldn't understand her because the girl next to her translated.

"Gakgak," said the girl with the twisted leg. "Kayak," the girl next to her repeated. "Kayak. Thunderbird. Men. Do the men come in the kayak or the thunderbird, Sasha?"

"Kayak," Sasha replied. "Men. Thunderbird. Men."

"What's this?" another girl asked.

"It looks like 'home,'" another girl said, puzzled.

"I guess I'm dumb, Sasha," the first girl said apologetically. "I don't get it. Is this a new story?"

The girls' heads remained bent, and Kate, curious, stood on tiptoe and peered over them to see what held so much of their attention.

Sasha was drawing in the sand. "Kayak," she said firmly, and a single line, curved up at both ends, appeared over three wavy, parallel lines. "Thunderbird." A few swift strokes and there was a pair of wings attached to a fierce hooked beak next to the kayak. "Men." A series of kinetic Y's with legs marched from kayak to thunderbird, three in all, where two other male figures waited. With a single sweep of her hand, all the drawings were enclosed in a perfect circle, almost encompassing the girls' toes. Another circle was drawn inside the first, perhaps two inches from the first one and perfectly concentric. There was grace and assurance in every stroke.

Sasha wasn't drawing with her finger, as Kate had thought at first. She bent forward to see more clearly and realized that the misshapen hand clutched a knife carved from ivory. It looked like a small scimitar, and the thing gleamed up at her in the dull light of the afternoon, smooth and shining from years of use. "Oh!" she exclaimed involuntarily. "How beautiful!"

There was a muffled communal shriek of surprise and the circle of girls exploded in every direction. Sasha would have run, too, but her bad leg folded beneath her and she lay panting in the sand. She had dropped the ivory knife and Kate reached for it.

"No!" Sasha cried.

"It's all right," Kate said quickly, kneeling next to her. "Here." She held the knife out and Sasha snatched it out of her hands, clutching it to her breast. "It's all right," Kate said again in a soothing voice. "I'm not going to hurt you. My name is Kate. What's yours?"

Sasha's eyes flickered beneath heavy lids. She was whimpering a little, and lay half in, half out of the water, which was rapidly soaking into her clothes.

Kate couldn't leave her like that. "Come on," she said, holding out her hand. "Let me help you up."

The girl cringed away from her, but Kate, moving slowly,

letting the girl see her every movement as it was made, put her hands under Sasha's arms and raised her to her feet. She cradled the girl's arm in a comforting hand and matched her steps to the girl's lurching ones. She was wet through, Kate noted with dismay. "Where do you live?" she asked, pitching her rough voice to be as nonthreatening as possible.

A small voice next to her made her jump. "She should go to Auntie's house. It's about six houses down. I'll show you."

Kate looked around to see the translator, a tiny, slender girl with long, tangled brown hair and a round face looking at her soberly.

"Hello," Kate said. "I'm Kate."

"I'm Becky," the girl replied. "You're not Anglo."

"No," Kate said. "Or at least not much." Becky's smile was shy, but it was a smile. Encouraged, Kate said, "I'm sorry I scared you. I was walking down the beach and I heard you guys and I walked over to take a look. What was that Sasha was doing with the knife?"

"Storyknifing," Becky said.

"Storyknifing? What's that?"

Becky looked up at Kate, her amazement written large on her face. "Didn't you storyknife when you were little?"

Kate shook her head. "No. I've never seen anything like it. I've seen art for sale in Anchorage, hell, I've seen art hung in the museum there that was drawn a lot worse than what I saw Sasha drawing down on the beach." At Becky's inquiring look, she said, "I heard you call her by name while I was watching her draw."

"Oh."

"So tell me about storyknifing."

Becky's brown eyes examined Kate in a way that made her feel as if she were being dissected in preparation for study

95

beneath a microscope. "It's just a game," she said at last. "A girl's game. Auntie showed us how. She said her mom showed her, and *her* mom showed *her*. We draw pictures in the sand, sometimes in the snow, and tell stories to each other. Up here."

Becky climbed the stoop and opened the door without knocking. "Auntie! Sasha fell down and got all wet!"

"Oh, that girl!" A tiny woman with a face whose features were almost swallowed up by the wrinkles on it shot out of the kitchen and buzzed around them like an infuriated bee. "Sasha," she said, her voice scolding but affectionate, "you naughty girl! What a mess! And you're shivering! Get out of those wet things this instant! Becky, take her down to the bathroom and run her a bath. There are clean towels in the linen closet. Scoot, scoot!"

Over her shoulder Becky said, "This is Kate, Auntie. She helped Sasha."

The bee turned to Kate. "Well, don't just stand there, you must be chilled through, come into the kitchen and have some tea."

"No, really," Kate said feebly, at the same time being swept into the old woman's irresistible wake. They went down a hallway and through a door into a large kitchen that took up half the square feet of the house and whose floor was covered in what looked like white straw. Kate stood still, ankle-deep in the stuff. "You look like you're busy, maybe I should go."

"Nonsense," the other woman said firmly, "come in this instant and sit down next to the stove. How did you find Sasha?"

Kate subsided meekly into the chair next to the oil stove. It gave out a warming, radiant heat and Kate realized how chilled she was. "Don't just sit there, take your jacket off," the older woman said. "I'm Olga Shapsnikoff, by the way."

"Kate," Kate said. "Kate Shugak."

Olga stopped short in mid-career. "Shugak? Any relation to Ekaterina Shugak?"

Kate was tempted to lie. "Yes," she said. "Ekaterina Shugak is my grandmother."

"Really." Olga busied herself with the teakettle, and her back looked somehow less than enthusiastic. Kate warmed to her.

"I attended a meeting chaired by Ekaterina at the last Raven convention," Olga said. "She certainly is a—" She hesitated, and looked over her shoulder. "She certainly is a strong woman."

The word you're looking for is "dictatorial," Kate thought. Also tyrannical, imperial and just plain pushy. She said nothing. Ekaterina might be all those things, but Ekaterina was her grandmother and this woman was a stranger. "Tell me about storyknifing," she said. "I've never seen a storyknife before. Is it an Aleut custom?"

After a long, thoughtful look that gave Kate the distinct impression that she had been tested and, thankfully, not found wanting, Olga smiled. "It's more of an Eskimo custom," she replied, turning back to the stove. "My grandmother was from Alakanuk."

As Olga boiled water and made tea, the rest of the girls from the circle on the beach drifted into the house one at a time, taking a seat around the large, scarred kitchen table, warming their hands around mugs of hot tea and casting shy, surreptitious glances at Kate. After a while Sasha lumbered in, dressed in clean, dry clothes, her skin flushed with the heat of her bath and her wet hair slicked back like a seal's. She sat down on the floor close to Olga's knees and took up a handful of the white straw.

"What is all this?" Kate asked, gesturing at the haystack with her mug.

"The girls and I are weaving baskets." Olga whipped a length of damp sheeting from the back of the table and displayed the beginnings of a dozen baskets that at first glance seemed to be made of cloth.

"Oh," Kate said, on a long note of discovery. "You're an Attuan basket weaver."

"Unalaskan, now," Olga said, her lips curling ever so slightly. One of the girls gave a giggle, quickly smothered.

Kate touched one of the tiny things. It was soft, even silken to the touch. The weaving was very fine, the stitches minute. None of the baskets were more than three inches in diameter. Each one had the same intricate pattern woven around its base in a different color of grass.

"'Baskets of grass which are both strong and beautiful,'" she said softly. She looked up at Olga. "Captain Cook wrote that in his log, when he visited Unalaska in 1778."

Becky sniffed, disdain sitting oddly on her young face. "The Unalaska baskets were very coarse."

"So I've read," Kate agreed. "The ones on Attu were supposed to be the best, weren't they?"

This time Olga sniffed, and being older and more experienced carried it off better than Becky had. It was a sound of profound disdain. "If you say so."

"I don't know anything about it really," Kate admitted, "except for what I've read about it. And I've seen the baskets in the museum in Anchorage, of course. How long does it take you to make one of these?"

"Six months," Olga said. "Maybe six years."

Kate looked at her incredulously. "It's true," Olga insisted. "It depends on how big the basket is. A basket two and a half inches high takes about forty hours. But when the old ones made shrouds, it could take years to finish just one. Would you like to try?"

"Making a shroud?"

Olga laughed. "We'll start you on a basket."

There was a shuffling around the table as each girl found her own basket. Half a dozen dark heads bent forward, identical intent expressions on each small face. Evidently this was serious business, and Kate said as much.

"One of these little baskets can bring as much as two hundred and fifty," Olga told her.

"Dollars?"

"Dollars," Olga confirmed with a twinkle in her eye.

Kate looked at the baskets the girls were working on with a new and growing respect. "This how you girls make your spending money?" Six heads nodded without looking up, six pairs of fingers worked steadily without missing a beat. Kate turned back to Olga and found a handful of the bleached grass under her nose.

"Peel the outer layers off, like this. You see?"

"Uh-huh," Kate lied. She got the definite feeling that Olga explained things one time and one time only.

"There are inner blades, here, and outer blades, what we call seconds. Keep them separate."

One blade of grass looked pretty much like another to Kate, but she sorted hers into what she prayed were the correct piles. "Okay."

"You split it, like this, with your thumbnail."

After nearly a month at sea on a crab boat, Kate didn't have much in the way of thumbnails and her first efforts were clumsy at best.

"All right," Olga said. "This is the spoke, and this is a

weaver. The spokes are the frame, and the weavers are twisted around the frame. Okay. You take a piece of grass and twist it. Here, I'll start yours for you. Remember, you work always from the bottom up, and clockwise."

"Who taught you how to do this. Auntie?"

"My grandmother, a little. The rest I taught myself by taking some old baskets apart."

"No one else does this anymore?"

"Very few. Many of the old weavers who were left died in the flu epidemic in 1919," Olga said, "and of course none of them told anyone else how they did their weaving."

"Why not?"

"Because every weaver had her own special weaving styles, and there was jealousy between the villages. Each one always wanted to be the best, so each one kept her ways secret from the others." Olga sighed a little. "Now they are all dead, and the weaving is almost dead, too."

"Not as long as you're alive, Auntie," Becky said, and the girls giggled.

"For which you should be glad," Olga told them, "or you wouldn't be able to buy that new Michael Jackson album. No," Olga told Kate, "dabble your fingers in the water first. The grass must be damp to work. Not too much! Only wet down as much as you are going to use at one time. You have to wrap up what you don't use, and it will mildew if you put it away damp."

After straining and sweating an hour, Kate produced her first weave, a tiny circle of clumsy stitches that nevertheless was recognizable as the beginning of a basket. "Good," Olga said. "Now keep going."

Easy for you to say, Kate thought. "You've got a lot of grass here," she said, nodding at the pile on the kitchen floor.

"Looks like enough to keep you weaving until next Christmas."

Olga shook her head and extended her arms in a circle, the tips of her fingers barely touching. "From this much grass, you get this many weavers." She put her right forefinger and thumb around her left wrist.

"That's all?"

"That's all," the old woman confirmed. "That's why it's important to pick the best grass."

"And where is the best grass?"

"Away from the salt water. Grass on the beach is too thick. It gets brittle after curing."

"So you pick in the hills?"

Olga nodded, her face bent over her basket, her expression absorbed as she conjured some especially intricate design out of the rim. "You learn where the good grass grows. If you keep picking in the same place the grass gets better."

"That's why we go back to Anua every year," Becky interpolated.

Kate broke a spoke. "Anua?"

Her voice must have sounded as startled as she felt because Becky cast her a curious glance. "Sure. It's where our family comes from."

"Oh." Kate began the arduous process of threading another spoke into the weaving, running through a mental list of questions to ask. She couldn't afford the appearance of prying or she would lose all the confidence she had gained so far. She recognized the investigator in her superseding the fellow tribal member and was momentarily ashamed of herself. But two men were missing, and probably dead and she didn't like Harry Gault so she said in a casual voice, "So if you're from Anua, why do you live in Unalaska?"

"It was the war," Becky said. "Tell her the story, Auntie."

"It was the war," Olga said. Her voice dropped into a rhythm, slipping into it so effortlessly and so seamlessly that Kate didn't notice it at once. "The Japanese soldiers came.

"Then the army came.
"The army moved all of the people from the islands.
"They put them in towns and in camps in Cook Inlet and Prince William Sound.
"It was too hot up there for the people.
"Many of the people died.
"After the war, the army brought us back.
"The people that were left wished they had died with the others.
"The houses were gone.
"The villages were gone.
"Even the ones where there had been no Japanese.
"The army said they destroyed them because they couldn't leave the villages for the Japanese to use.
"We couldn't go back.
"There weren't enough of us.
"There was nothing to go back to.
"So now we live in a few villages instead of many.
"That's all."

The room was silent but for the rustle of grass. Kate kept her head bent over her basket. When she could speak, she said, "Do you ever go back to Anua?"

"Sure," Becky said, at the same time Olga said, "No."

The girl's eyes widened. Olga said easily, "Only for the grass. In June or July, when it is ready to pick. But mostly we use Chinaman's grass, raffia, that we buy from Outside. It takes too long to pick and cure the rye grass." The old woman smiled. "And the tourists can't tell the difference."

Kate grinned. Before she could reply, Sasha said suddenly, "Home."

They all looked at her, seated on the floor, her crippled leg again twisted awkwardly beneath her. She still had the ivory knife, and with it she traced a pattern on the old linoleum floor, the yellowed ivory of the old knife looking odd against the cracked paisley pattern. Her brown eyes were bright and alert, the most alive features in that blunted face. "Kayak. Men. Thunderbird. Men. Home."

"That's the same story she was telling on the beach this morning," Becky told Olga. "What does it mean?"

Olga shrugged, and leaned forward to pluck the storyknife from Sasha's now limp fingers. "I don't know. What do any of Sasha's stories mean?"

"But her stories always make sense. Auntie," Becky protested. "Somehow, they always do. You just have to figure them out."

"Thunderbird," Sasha said clearly. "Men. Kayak. Men. Home."

"See? She knows what we're talking about."

Olga looked at Becky. "The storyknife is just a toy, Becky. It makes Sasha happy to play with it. That's all."

Becky's mouth closed and she bent back over her basket, a tinge of red creeping up into her cheeks.

"Tell me about the storyknife, Auntie," Kate suggested into the uncomfortable silence that followed. "I've never seen one before. It's beautiful."

Olga looked down at the ivory knife she held in her hands.

"My grandmother gave it to me. My great-uncle made it for her when she was a little girl. It's a toy. A girl's toy. We use it to draw stories in the sand, and in the snow."

"Where did it come from? The custom, I mean?"

Olga shrugged. "Some people say it used to be a real knife. That the Eskimos used it to cut snow into blocks for igloos. All I know is I got this one from my mother. My mother got it from her mother. Other girls had them when I was a child. It was a custom." She handed the storyknife to Kate.

Kate accepted it in reverent hands. The handle was carved with the stylized likeness of a sea otter floating on his back. In spite of the wear and tear caused by at minimum four pairs of grubby little hands, each individual whisker stood out on his tiny face. He stared up at Kate, expectant. The ivory seemed to grow heavier in her hand. Kate cleared her throat. "Are they always made from ivory?"

"No. Some are made from bone or wood."

"It's a beautiful thing, Auntie," Kate said, handing it back. "And valuable. It should be in a museum."

"And would a museum take it out and play with it?" Olga demanded, and gave a snort. "Its spirit would die, locked up in a place where it was never touched. Here the girls play with it, and it tells them stories."

Which made it something more than just a toy, Kate thought. She looked down at the rapidly shredding beginning of her basket, and said ruefully, "I don't seem to be doing very well at this, Auntie. I guess I'm just a cultural illiterate."

"Nonsense," Olga said briskly. "It takes practice, like anything else. You will take some grass with you when you leave, so you can work at it on your own."

Wonderful, Kate thought, but said meekly, "Thank you, Auntie."

"And now more tea? And some *alodiks*?"

"*Alodiks*?" Kate said.

The old woman looked at her reprovingly. "You have no Aleut?"

Kate shook her head.

"Because your grandmother wanted you to?" Olga guessed shrewdly, and laughed, a loud, cackling laugh, at Kate's expression. Kate was relieved when Olga turned to the stove, and even more relieved when *alodiks* proved to be nothing more than fried bread. A few minutes later Olga put a plateful of the stuff in the middle of the table, puffed up and golden brown. Everyone around the table made a concerted grab, not excepting Kate.

"There were killer whales in the bay this morning, Auntie," one of the girls said around a mouthful of fried bread.

"Ahhhhh," Olga said. "Killer whales in the bay." The smile faded from her face and she shook her head gravely.

"What does it mean?"

"Killer whales in the bay?"

"Yes. Do you know what it means?"

"I know only what everyone knows." Olga worked her next few stitches without speaking. The girls ceased their giggling and whispering, and as the silence gathered and grew, Kate had the feeling of a curtain about to go up.

When she spoke again, Olga's voice fell again into a kind of singsong, with a full-stop pause at the end of each sentence. It was subtle but clear. It wasn't as if Olga banged a drum on the downbeat at the end of every line, but Becky and her sister began nodding their heads slightly to the beat. Kate had noticed a similar kind of cadence to Olga's story of the Aleuts' exile and repatriation during and after World War II, and now consciously scanned the old woman's words for rhythm. She found it, and repetition, and internal rhymes, and alliteration. Without moving, the girls seemed to draw tighter together in their circle, intent, absorbed, almost hypnotized, acolytes hanging on the words of their priestess.

"When killer whales come to a bay with a village," Olga chanted, "they come hungry for someone's spirit.

"When the killer whales come
"To a bay with a village
"Someone is going to die.
"When the killer whales come
"To a bay with a village
"The people know.
"When the killer whales come
"To a bay with a village
"It won't be long.
"Maybe one month.
"Maybe two.
"When the killer whales come
"Someone dies in that bay.
"When the killer whales come.
"That's all."

As she spoke the last words, Olga looked straight at Kate. She held her gaze for a long moment, before her eyes dropped to the scar on Kate's throat. The skin there began to itch beneath that intent gaze. Kate held perfectly still. "That was a beautiful story, Auntie," she said. "You're a poet."

Olga laughed, a loud robust laugh, and the priestess was gone and her acolytes, too, on the gust of merriment. "It's just an old legend," she said, dropping back into prose. "I'm a good Christian missionary's daughter, myself. I don't believe any of that stuff."

Kate burst out laughing, and the girls joined in again.

As she rose to leave, Kate hesitated, not wanting to trespass but the memory of those graceful, swooping sand drawings haunting her. "About Sasha."

Olga's face was expressionless. "What about her?"

"Has she seen a doctor? There might be—"

"There is nothing," Olga said flatly. "Her mother drank too much."

• • •

"Where does Sasha live?" Kate asked Becky outside. "With family, parents, what?" She was determined to do something, anything. Anyone who could draw like Sasha was not, could not be entirely beyond help, fetal alcohol syndrome baby or not.

She turned her head to find Becky looking at her with surprise. "What?"

Becky jerked a thumb over her shoulder, at the house behind them. "Sasha lives right here, Kate. Auntie is Sasha's mom."

CHAPTER 6

THE HARBOR'S DOCK space was so limited that the *Avilda* was again third in a row of boats rafted four deep. The next morning the tide was at slack and it was a long way down to the first boat tied to the dock. There are worse things in life than hanging in the pitch-dark from a forty-foot ladder, trying to find a foothold on the icy railing of a boat being tossed up and down in the enthusiastic embrace of a spirited groundswell. Offhand, Kate couldn't think of one.

She shut her ears to the rush of water, the smack of the swell on the bottom of a hundred hulls, the murmur of idling engines, the shout of impatient skippers. Moving one limb at a time, she felt her cautious way down to the next rung on the ladder and extended a foot in what she prayed was the general direction of the boat. A barnacle crunched beneath the foot still on the ladder, the sole of her boot slid across the rung, her balance shifted and one hand pulled free. She made a wild grab for the ladder and by a miracle caught it.

She pressed her forehead against cold metal and scratchy barnacle, her heart pounding in her ears, gasping for breath. Water rushed in among the pilings with a chuckling sound. Her mouth tightened into an unseen snarl and she swiveled on the rung, bent her knees, let go and jumped blind. For a moment she was suspended in midair, and then she hit the deck awkwardly. Instinct took over and she tucked her head and rolled forward in a somersault. Her butt hit something hard and she stopped rolling, her feet falling forward with a thump.

For a moment she just lay there, panting. She heard a noise from the boat's cabin like someone was about to come on deck and she shot to her feet and made for the opposite railing. The rest of the journey was by comparison a piece of cake; all she had to do was straddle the tied-together railings of the two boats with one leg and swing her other leg over. Always supposing the boats were of equal size, which they often weren't, in which case she had to either climb up or jump down or both. When she slithered onto the *Avilda*'s heaving deck she knew a moment of pure triumph.

She was making breakfast when Andy emerged from their stateroom, rumpled and yawning. He peered over her shoulder at the eggs scrambled with cheese and onions and green chile and bits of shredded tortilla. "Looks good. Smells great."

"You eat eggs?" she said, eyes wide. "Eggs come from chickens. Come to think of it, eggs are chickens, before they hatch. You might be chowing down on something's soul here, messing up their *prima* all to hell and gone. Maybe you should reconsider." She gave him a big smile. "I could pour you a bowl of cereal."

Ignoring her, he poured himself a cup of coffee. "Thought it was Ned's turn to cook."

"He's not back on board yet."

Andy looked surprised. "I thought we were taking this tide."

"So did I." Kate sprinkled in some garlic powder and gave the eggs a final stir before turning off the burner and removing the skillet from the stove.

"Harry'll be pissed," Andy said, sounding satisfied at the prospect.

"He's not back yet, either." The toast popped out and Kate

buttered it with a lavish hand.

Andy stopped with his cup halfway to his mouth. "Seth?"

"Nope."

There was a short silence. Into his coffee mug Andy said, "This isn't a very well-run boat, is it, Kate?"

"Nope."

"I mean it, I'm getting off, soon as I find something else."

Kate shrugged. "You should have been on my last boat." And only, she thought but didn't say. "The skipper had a loudspeaker mounted on the foredeck and wired into a microphone on the bridge so he could talk to the crew on deck whenever he wanted to, and he wanted to all the time. Yap, yap, yap, from how to grab a buoy with a boat hook to how to chop bait to how to fill a bait jar to how to tie door ties to how to sort crab. This guy never but never shut up." Kate ladled eggs onto a plate and paused, remembering. "He had this real high, squeaky voice that sounded ten times worse amplified. It drove everybody crazy."

"What happened?"

Kate shrugged again. "One day the speaker didn't work. For a while the skipper didn't notice it. We'd look up at the bridge and he'd be standing at the wheel, yapping away into the mike, but we couldn't hear a word. It was like the difference between heaven and hell. Then he gave somebody an order and of course nobody heard him and he realized something was wrong. He traced the wires to the speaker and found somebody'd cut them."

Andy grinned. "How much do you know about electronics, Kate?"

Kate handed him a heaping plate. "Shut up and eat your breakfast." She made herself a plate, scraped the remaining eggs to one side of the frying pan and stacked the rest of the toast next to them. She covered the whole thing to keep it warm and sat down to eat. She, too, wondered where the rest of the crew was, and what they were doing. If Harry old buddy and his two chosen sons were going to make this vanishing act a habit, she was going to have to figure out how to tail them through Dutch Harbor's immense metropolitan district without getting spotted. The prospect did not delight her. She was good, but she wasn't that good.

They were on their second cup of coffee when Harry, Ned and Seth finally showed up. Ned and Seth were carrying suitcases, one each, the shiny silver kind that photographers use to pack their lenses into.

Kate eyed the suitcases. "Been Christmas shopping?"

"You could say that," Ned said, almost pleasantly, which made Kate wonder if there was something wrong with her hearing.

"Yep, visions of sugarplums dance in our heads," Seth added, and the three of them burst out laughing, even Seth.

They were in a wonderful mood in an exclusive sort of way, nudging each other, exchanging winks, sharing muffled comments and chuckles. The only thing worse than this crew surly was this crew merry. Andy finished his coffee and, reassured by an expansive Harry Gault that the *Avilda* was staying where she was for the time being, went uptown, probably to work on sniffing out a new berth. Kate put her dishes in the dishwasher and went out on deck to coil shots and chop bait, and plot a chance to locate and find out what was inside the shiny silver suitcases brought on board that morning.

She was still on deck when a pump started below and began emptying the bilge into the harbor. After a while the pump stopped, but in the growing daylight the oily sheen growing from their hull was easy to spot, until Ned came forward with a bottle of detergent and squirted it over the side. It cut through the oil and the sheen floated off. Ned grinned at her. "Slicker'n snot."

"Thought we weren't supposed to pump the bilge out into the harbor," she said in a neutral voice, eyes on the line she was coiling. "Turn the place into a sewer if we all did it."

He shrugged. "Ain't my harbor."

He went aft, and Kate thought that maybe Andy had the right idea.

● ● ●

When the *Avilda* arrived back out on the fishing grounds Kate was surprised and relieved to find all their gear right where it was supposed to be. The take had decreased, but the lines were intact, the netting unslashed and the buoys whole. It was more than she had expected.

On their two previous trips they had averaged a hundred tanners per pot (or at least that was their average on pots that had not previously been picked). If the average weight of *bairdi* was two and a half pounds, at $ 1.50 per pound that meant each pot was worth $375. Her crew share, eight percent, had been thirty dollars a pot, and they had been picking a minimum of forty pots a day. Kate began to feel cheated whenever a pot came up half empty, and she got downright surly when most of what was in the pots proved to be garbage.

Apparently Harry Gault felt the same way. He gave orders not to bait and reset the pots as they were pulled, but instead to stack them on deck. Naturally the deck boss didn't bother telling the rest of the crew what the plan was.

Andy finished coiling and stacking a shot of polypro and wandered over in Kate's direction. "What's going on?" he asked in a low voice.

Kate ran a final loop through the frame of the last pot and tested the line. It held firm. She gave a satisfied nod. "Looks like the skipper's finally noticed we've lost the crab. Best guess? We're going prospecting."

Andy looked confused. "Prospecting?"

"Set a pot here, there. Try to find where the tanners went."

• • •

For the next week that's what they did, cruising up and down the Chain, setting a few pots, pulling them to examine the contents, meandering a little farther west, a little farther south to repeat the process in untested waters. Occasionally the fog would clear and a smoking, snowcapped volcano would loom up off the bow. With the amount of weather that swirled in and out in a twenty-four-hour period, it was hard for the crew to tell just what direction they were traveling in, and of course Harry Gault was as garrulous and forthcoming as always, which meant that the only time he opened his mouth was to bark an order.

So immersed was she in her role as deckhand that Kate began to be concerned over the lack of crab in each pot and the subsequent lack of crab in the hold. The paychecks from her last two trips out were folded away into the pocket of her jeans, where they made a nice, solid weight. Her sleep had begun to be disturbed by dreams of a new truck, a larger generator for the homestead. Maybe even a satellite dish. She liked to watch MTV and VH-1 when she visited the Roadhouse, catch up on the latest in music. She used to sing

113

and play the guitar. Singing was out now, as that baby raper's knife had almost taken out her vocal cords, but she still loved music, and her taste was eclectic to say the least. She had recently become a fan of k. d. lang's, and remembered suddenly that on satellite you got The Nashville Network, too. She reached inside her pocket to touch the two folded slips of paper, and dreamed on.

She woke up to realize it was coming up on dinnertime and her turn to cook. She straightened and stretched. The gray-green gulf stretched out endlessly in every direction, a snowcapped peak with a faint plume rising from it floated in a ring of fog off the port beam, and Ned was emptying a pot on deck.

He was about to toss its contents over the side and she raised her voice. "Hold it, Ned."

"Nothing but garbage," Ned growled when she came up next to him.

Kate sorted through the pot's contents. "We've got four red kings—"

"Not in season."

"—a chicken halibut—"

"Which can't weigh fifteen pounds."

"—and a half-dozen Dungeness. Big ones, too," Kate said admiringly.

"What you want them for?" Ned asked suspiciously.

Kate gave him her sweetest smile. "I'm on dinner tonight."

She found the biggest cooking pot in the galley, filled it with water and set it on a burner turned on high, and went below to assemble the ingredients for the rest of the meal. The industrial-size refrigerator and freezer were located in a small room set down into the hull behind the hold and the engine room. She descended the ladder with reluctance. She hated the small, square, walk-in freezer in the storeroom. The door was so heavy, she was always afraid it would swing shut behind her, that the bar across the outside would fall into its bracket and she would be locked inside, left to spend eternity between the prime rib and the pork chops. The thought alone was enough to send a shudder down her spine, and she snatched up a can of lard and scuttled out of the freezer, kicking the door shut behind her with an explosive breath of relief. An armful of salad makings out of the refrigerator and dinner was as good as done.

She busied herself in the galley as the *Avilda* beat to windward, and her crew that night sat down to a dinner of boiled king and Dungeness crab, halibut deep-fried in beer batter, a mountain of mashed potatoes and, for Andy, a tossed green salad. Ned, Seth and Harry took one look and fell into their seats. Pawing through the pile of cutlery Kate had stacked in the center of the table, each man found the pair of pliers that suited him best and began cracking crab with gusto. Mayonnaise mustachioed their mouths, melted butter ran down their chins, crab juice ran down their arms and soaked the newspapers Kate had spread on the floor, and the empty shells piled steadily higher in the emptied cooking pot she had placed in the center of the table for just that purpose.

When they were through, not a leg or a claw or a shoulder of crab was left, nor was a single piece of the halibut. Harry sat back and patted his belly, expressing his feelings with a loud, satisfied belch. This appeared to be the general consensus. "Jesus, that was good," Seth said, and even Ned nodded grudgingly. Overwhelmed by such enthusiastic, unqualified approval, Kate decided she could get to like these guys, given time. Say about a hundred years. She stretched. "Who cleans up?"

Three thumbs jerked at Andy. Kate grinned at his woebegone expression. "Think I'll turn in. Nighty-night."

"Me, too," Harry said, yawning. "Ned, you take the first watch; Seth, you take the second. Roust me out if there's trouble."

Kate hit the rack and fell instantly into a deep, dreamless sleep.

• • •

A thump on the door brought her wide awake. "What?" she croaked. There was another thump and she raised her voice. "What, dammit!"

Harry's voice was already receding down the hallway. "Roll out. We're making ice."

She groped for her watch and saw that it was barely midnight. Her head fell back on the pillow with a thump. "Oh, shit." An instant later she was up and yanking on her clothes. Andy's face peered down at her with a bewildered expression. "What's going on?"

"We're making ice."

"What's making ice?"

"Get up on deck and you'll see. And, Andy?" She met his eyes. "Put on *all* your clothes."

A collection of blunt instruments waited for them in the galley. Kate took a baseball bat and, since he looked confused, chose one of the smaller sledgehammers for Andy. "Can you lift that? Show me. Okay. Let's go."

He followed her, the words of protest dying in his throat when he saw what waited for them on deck.

The weather, predictably, had worsened while they slept. The *Avilda* labored sluggishly up and down the swells, crashing into waves twelve to twenty feet high. That was nothing new, but the cold was.

The temperature had dropped as the weather worsened, and in the time it took the salt spray to fly through the air and hit the deck it had frozen into a multitude of tiny pellets that skipped and crackled across the deck, sounding like Rice Krispies after pouring the milk in. The spray froze to everything it touched, to the deck itself, to the pots stacked on that deck, to the mast and boom, to the rigging attached to the mast and boom, to the superstructure of the *Avilda*'s cabin. Every inch of the surface of the boat that was above water was encased in a sheet of ice. It was already inches thick on the bow and mast, and thickening rapidly everywhere else.

"Sweet Jesus H. Christ on a crutch," Andy said, his voice sounding awed even over the storm. It was the first time Kate had ever heard him swear. "We look like the fucking *Flying Dutchman*."

Kate cocked her head. It might be her imagination, but she thought she detected a hint of strain in the movement of the *Avilda*'s hull; she seemed to wallow through the next swell, puffing and panting as she went. Kate advanced to the boom across a terrifyingly icy deck, braced her feet against the raised lip of the hatch, raised the bat and brought it down as hard as she could. Her feet slipped and she felt the strike reverberate back up her arms. Gritting her teeth, she struck again. A large chunk of ice cracked and fell to the deck. A swell passed beneath the hull, the deck slanted and the chunk of ice slid overboard. She slipped again and almost followed it. From the corner of her eye she saw Andy, openmouthed, look from her to Ned, who was hammering at the bow with a sledgehammer twice the size of the one he held, to Seth, who was perched precariously on the catwalk in front of the bridge, trying to beat the windows clear with a three-foot piece of rebar. "Beat on it," she growled, and wound up for another swing.

"Beat on the ice?"

"Yes. Hammer at it. Break it off and throw it overboard."

"Why?"

The bat thumped into the mast again. "Because it's heavy. Because we don't have jack shit in the hold. Because if we let the ice build up, we'll get top-heavy, and if we get too top-heavy it'll make the ship roll over and capsize, and if we capsize we'll go in the water, and if we go in the water, we won't have time enough to drown before the hypothermia sets in." Because the Bering Sea's just looking for a reason to give Harry Gault what for, she thought. Kate had four years of college, a year's additional training in the most sophisticated police technology, and she'd worked five years in Anchorage, what passed for a city in Alaska. In spite of it all, her Aleut heritage, generations of living on and from the ocean, told her that the sea itself had risen up in outrage at Harry Gault's mean-spirited, spiteful, venomous revenge on Johansen and the *Daisy Mae*. She didn't think this, she would have laughed out loud if someone had told it to her, but she was convinced of it on some deep, instinctual, atavistic level. Agudar, Master Hunter, had called down the North Wind and called up the sea to punish them, to bring the forces of nature back into balance. "Beat on it, dammit!" she told Andy through clenched teeth. "Beat on it! Break it off!"

Her snarl snapped Andy out of his trance. He closed his mouth, raised his sledgehammer and advanced toward the fo'c'sle. Over the roar of the wind, Kate heard a crunching thud, a pause, another thud, another pause. Someone swore. The thudding began again and settled into a kind of rhythm, uncertain at first, a little ragged, but maintaining a dogged

118

persistence. After a while Kate ceased to hear anything but the slap of the hull into the sea, the cackle and skitter of freezing spray and the roar of the wind all around.

The bat rose and fell, rose and fell. Ice shattered and broke and as quickly froze over again. The *Avilda* groaned through the waves, creaking all the way down her hull under the strain. Kate groaned through the swing of the bat, her shoulders creaking beneath the weight, the strain. This wasn't work, this wasn't making a buck, this was survival, plain and simple. Numbness began in the tips of her fingers and crept up through her hands to her wrists and arms. Behind her came the crash of ice as Seth broke a large piece free from the catwalk. Ice shattered from the bow and splashed into the water below. Andy worked his way up one railing and down the other, as behind him a new layer froze and thickened. The baseball bat beat its way with monotonous regularity from one side of the fo'c'sle and back again. The wind made the rigging hum, sharp needles of freezing spray pierced her skin, the deck was icy and treacherous beneath her feet.

Kate had ceased to care. The bat rose and fell, rose and fell. The ice began to take on personality, to become an animate force, malevolent, vindictive, relentless, maniacal, homicidal. No matter how hard or how often the bat fell, the ice reappeared inexorably, inevitably behind it, enfolding the *Avilda* in a cold embrace, enveloping the crew in wintry arms, its purpose a deadly seduction whose end was death.

The ever-increasing weight of this deadly seduction slowed the movement of both ship and crew. With each sluggish list the layer of ice grew thicker and the *Avilda* took longer to right herself again. With each lift of her arms it seemed to take Kate longer to bring the bat down, harder to exert the force necessary to break off the ice. She felt lethargic, torpid, apathetic. She was so tired. All she wanted was to find somewhere to lie down and go to sleep forever. It didn't matter if the bunk was wet or dry or frozen over. She just wanted to close her eyes.

She came alert with a jerk that pulled her out of her stupor, and blinked her eyes against the ice forming on her lashes. Think, she told herself. Just think for a minute.

The engine coughed once, hesitated for one eternal moment and again picked up the beat. The vibrations pulsated up through the deck into her feet, a life-giving cadence counting off. Kate refused to think of it as counting down.

Cadence. Meter. Stress. Poetry. In another life she used to read poetry. What poetry did she used to read? Her mind was blank, like the engine forgetting how to run for that one terrifying second. Words finally came. "The ice was here, the ice was there, the ice was all around." The words of the Ancient Mariner sprang unbidden to mind and Kate shook her head doggedly. What else? "Full fathom five thy father lies; of his bones are coral made." No. Definitely not. "Sunset and evening star, and one clear call for me."

She stopped the bat in mid-swing, brought it down to rest on the deck and leaned on it, letting her head hang, ignoring the bite of the freezing spray, the icy fingers of the wind, taking long, deep, steadying breaths.

When she raised the bat again, it was to the four-four, four-three beat of ballads. "East is East, and West is West, and never the twain shall meet." "A French cocked hat on his forehead and a bunch of lace at his chin." "One if by land, and two if by sea; and I on the opposite shore will be." "I sprang to the stirrup and Joris and he, I galloped, Dirk galloped, we all galloped three."

She wondered why she had never noticed before how so

many ballads were written on horseback. The bat was coming down steadily now, in its own asymmetrical rhythm, batting out a tattoo of endurance, a measure of survival. When she got home, if she got home, she could write a ballad of her own. A bat in my hand and ice at my feet, and I in Dutch Harbor will Jack Morgan meet, ready his head into marshmallow beat, sheer satisfaction was never so sweet. She laughed, an involuntary snort of real amusement, surprising herself and astounding Andy, who paused with his sledgehammer in the air to look over at her with incredulous eyes. Longfellow she wasn't. She wasn't even Dr. Seuss.

Hours later, days later, years later, she felt rather than heard someone shouting. After a moment, she realized they were shouting at her. She looked up, dazed, to see Andy reaching for her. As if from a great distance she saw his hand close on her shoulder. He gave her a hard shake and she couldn't feel it. "Kate?"

She tried to shrug his hand away. Had to keep swinging. Had to beat the ice. Had to keep the *Avilda* with her head up and her feet down. "'He would answer to "Hi!" or to any loud cry,'" she muttered.

He peered at her, his young face red and chapped with frostbite. "Kate! Are you all right?"

"Of course I'm all right," she said petulantly, shrugging again beneath his hand. "What do you want?"

"We've stopped making ice. You can quit now."

Like coming out of a trance, Kate woke to the realization of a deck no longer canting so drastically beneath her feet that she had to fear losing her foothold and sliding overboard. There was no noise from the engine, from which she painstakingly formulated the hypothesis that it had been shut down. No spray hit the deck.

The gusting wind had died to a breeze that barely rippled the surface of the water, as if the Cradle of the Winds were saying, What, me? Hurt you? How could you think such a thing? It was all just a little joke, teehee. You can relax now, catch some Z's. Sleep tight, and don't let those bedbugs bite.

Kate didn't believe a word of it but she was too tired to express her distrust. "Where are we?"

"Some island," Andy said, his voice weary. "Some bay on some island. I didn't ask."

"When killer whales come into a bay it means someone is going to die," Kate said.

"What?" Andy looked closer at her. "You look like hell, Kate. Hit the rack. I'll stow these." He reached for the bat. She resisted for a moment, and then let go so suddenly he staggered back a step. "Go on," he said, recovering his balance. "Go to bed."

Her mind searched tiredly for the correct response. When she spoke her tongue felt thick in her mouth. "Who's on watch?"

"We're on the hook, Kate," he said patiently. "We're anchored up in a bay on some island."

"A bay on some island," Kate repeated. "Did I tell you about the killer whales?"

"Yes, you told me." He turned her firmly in the direction of the galley door. "Go to bed."

She twisted her mouth into the semblance of a smile and he winced away from it. "Isn't Alaska just the greatest place?"

In the galley she stumbled into Ned and Seth coming down from the bridge, Harry behind them. As weary as she was the expression on their faces stopped her in her tracks. "What's wrong?"

The two men exchanged glances. "Another boat got caught

in the same storm."

"Which one?"

Again that exchange of glances. "The *Daisy Mae*."

A sick dread grew inside her. "And?"

Seth shook his head, his gaze somber. "They were able to get off a distress call, and their Loran numbers. The Coast Guard responded but by the time they got there, there was nothing."

"They recover the bodies?"

He shook his head again. "Then we have to go," Kate said. "They might have had time to get into their survival suits. We have to go help look. We have to," she insisted at his disbelieving look. "We have to look for them. They'd look for us."

"We barely made it this far," Harry growled. "The Coasties are on the scene, and half a dozen other boats. We go back out there and they're liable to have to come looking for *us*."

She couldn't stop the words. "You make a habit of not looking for fishermen lost at sea."

Suddenly it was very still in the galley. A dark red flush rose up from Harry's collar to flood his face. He stared at her, his lips drawn back from his teeth. She met his look squarely, knowing her contempt was obvious, unable to disguise it. From the corner of one eye she saw him raise one clenched fist, and waited with a curious kind of detachment to see what would happen next.

Seth caught Harry's elbow. With a growled obscenity Harry whipped around. Their eyes locked and for a moment, just for a moment, Harry froze. Seth said nothing, just looked at him. Breaking the spell, Harry yanked his arm free and shouldered past Seth, leaving Kate standing alone, unanswered, exhausted and sick at heart.

She shook off her paralysis long enough to wobble down

the passageway and fumble the door open to her stateroom. Her rain gear snapped and was easily discarded and she toed her boots off, but for some reason her sweater just wouldn't come over her head. She looked down at her hands. They were curled in imitation of her grip on the baseball bat. She couldn't straighten them. She couldn't even feel them. They were incapable of gripping the hem of her sweater.

It said much for her state of mind that she was unalarmed. She tucked her hands into her armpits, rolled into her bunk fully dressed, curled up in a ball and fell into a fitful, restless sleep, to dream the same dream over and over and over again, white fog and green water and thickening ice and a sinking boat and drowning crewmen. The last boat to sink was the *Avilda*, and the last drowning crewman's face was her own.

● ● ●

Her eyes snapped open and she stared into the darkness. She lay still, listening, trying to figure out what it was that had woken her. She would have bet every dime the *Avilda* had earned her that nothing short of a nuclear holocaust could have gotten between her and the land of Nod that night.

As usual on the Chain, the weather had done a volte-face and the slight swell was barely perceptible. The wind had died completely. The *Avilda* rode calmly at anchor in her bay on some island like a car in a parking lot. Kate had just decided that Andy's snoring must have woken her when a thump reverberated down the starboard side of the hull, the side her bunk was on, followed by a distant splash, a splash that sounded exactly like oars hitting water.

She rose with an effort, her body aching from the bones out. She sidled into the passageway, pausing when she saw that the door to Seth and Ned's room was ajar. She pushed it open a bit farther and peered around it. Their bunks were empty. She took a chance and opened the skipper's door. He, too, was gone. In stocking feet she padded swiftly to the galley and over to the starboard side door to peer out the window.

In the faint light of the stars Kate could detect the outline of the island. There was something familiar about its shape, and she studied it, brows puckering, before a movement below drew her gaze down to the water level. She stared intently, her eyes becoming accustomed to the darkness, and caught the movement again.

It was oars, oars attached to the *Avilda*'s skiff, a skiff that should be stowed upside down on the aft cabin roof at this moment. Remembering something Abel had taught her about making out indistinct, distant objects in the dark, she shifted her gaze a fraction to the right. On her peripheral vision the skiff registered clearly. It was heading toward the island, and there were three men in it.

Kate thought rapidly. The life rafts were out, she would never be able to deflate a life raft and repack it into its barrel without being caught. Besides, with Harry Gault at the helm she wanted both life rafts right where they were. Her hands clenched. Dammit, she *had* to know what was going on on that island, what Harry and Ned and Seth were up to.

She heard Jack's voice again, so carefully nonchalant. "There are survival suits aboard the *Avilda*, aren't there?"

Without stopping to think, because if she'd thought about it for even five seconds she never would have done it, she whipped around and headed for the opposite side of the galley and the locker beneath the bench next to the galley table. In the darkness she fumbled for the finger hole. She didn't dare turn on a light for fear it would be seen from the skiff. She hooked the hole at last, pulled the seat cover up and out and felt around inside for one of the plastic-wrapped packages, the one that had been opened before.

She had been looked at a little sardonically when she had insisted, her first day on board, on trying on one of the survival suits, but it was a good thing she had. It was bulky, made of a thick synthetic material that reminded her of nothing so much as woven polypropylene, with a multitude of zips and snaps and pull-tabs for an inflating collar and a buddy belt and a helicopter ring and who knew what else. She would never have been able to fumble her way into it in the dark if she hadn't done it at least once in daylight. As it was, she fought to get the right fingers into the right sections of the divided mitts and prayed the zip flap and the hood were properly fastened.

Opening the galley door, carefully muffling any sound that might carry across the water to the cursing men just now working the skiff off where it had caught on a reef, she stepped across to the railing and with great courage and no brains lowered herself over the side and into the water.

A body submerged in water loses body heat twenty-four times faster than it does in air of the same temperature. Kate's inconvenient memory produced this interesting fact at exactly the same moment the chill waters of the Bering Sea closed over her body. Cold, cold, it was so cold. Her hands and feet, which had already taken enough abuse that night, went numb instantly. Swearing at Gault, swearing at Jack, swearing at herself, she struck out for shore, struggling to keep her head up and her face out of the water.

The *Avilda* was anchored half a mile offshore. The tide was almost in and the distance seemed endless. The water lapped at her chin. She alternated a breaststroke with a dog-paddle and concentrated on breathing while trying not to splash.

Once her knee scraped against a rock too close to the surface, and she knew a moment of terror that the suit had been breached. Ahead of her she heard a scrap of muttered conversation, the grating sound of the skiff's hull as it was drawn up the shore, the crunch of sand beneath boots. Galvanized, she struck out for shore.

One kicking toe touched bottom, another, and she stood up and waded out, crouching in the water as long as she could so the water pouring off her would make as little noise as possible. Once on the beach, she stopped to catch her breath and listen. The sound of footsteps crunching through crusted snow floated back to her clearly on the still morning air. Trying to keep up with their pace so as to disguise the sound of her own steps, she began to walk behind them.

If Jack could see her now. This was a little different from tailing someone through the greater metropolitan area of Dutch Harbor, or downtown Anchorage, for that matter. Dripping and numb, she smiled into the darkness. Unzipping her mitts and freeing her hands, she moved forward cautiously, feeling her way up over the lip of the beach and into the thick grass. The sound of the men's footsteps began to fade, and afraid she was going to lose them she quickened her pace. Something tripped her and she lost her balance. The heavy survival suit made her clumsy and she fell. Something caught her and held, for just a moment, before it gave way and she was tumbling, down in the dark. She hit hard, and lay, feeling bruised and shaken, staring up at a hole in the world through which she could see stars twinkling. She gave an experimental wriggle. Material rustled beneath her. Feeling around with an inquiring hand, she touched tarpaulin. She looked back up at the hole and realized why the outline of the island had looked familiar. "Anua! We're on goddam Anua!"

At that moment she heard the sound of a distant engine, and for a single panicked moment thought the men had doubled back on her, returned to the *Avilda* and were leaving the island without her. She leapt to her feet, and recognized the sound of an airplane engine. Extremities numb from the cold water, body bruised from the fall, self exhausted from fighting the ice storm, all were forgotten as she yanked open the *barabara's* door. The sound of the airplane grew louder and Kate turned and headed for the airstrip at a smart clip, the thudding of her feet through the dry grass and snow covered by the noise of two engines on a short final. This time she didn't stumble. She was in familiar territory and she knew where she was going.

She topped the little rise and crouched immediately behind a clump of dead rye grass. A twin-engine Navaho was touching down to a landing on the hard-packed snow of the strip. Kate immediately stretched out flat on her stomach and prayed they hadn't seen her come crashing up while they were still in the air.

The Navaho bounced twice before rolling out to a stop next to the gas tank. Two men got out. The three men from the *Avilda* advanced to meet them. Nobody shook hands. Kate, cursing the lack of cover and the bright orange of her survival suit, strained to hear something, anything.

"Have you got it?" she thought she heard Harry say. He was answered by a low laugh. One of the men returned to the plane and produced a suitcase. A thickset figure Kate recognized as Ned produced two suitcases of his own, shiny silver suitcases that gleamed even in the predawn light. Shiny silver suitcases so well chaperoned that she hadn't been able to lay her hands on them for the past seven days.

One man each from boat and plane went to the gas tank

to connect the hose to the Navaho's wing tanks and refuel the plane. The other three squatted down on their haunches, produced flashlights and opened two of the suitcases. One was filled with a lot of something white, the other with a lot more of something green.

"*Yes*," Kate hissed. She was filled with a rush of fierce triumph. "Gotcha, you sonsabitches."

Kate harbored no illusions about honor among thieves. With leverage like this, it was only a matter of time before she got one crew member to roll over on the others and finally tell what had happened to Alcala and Brown. "*Yes*," she said again, her satisfaction as cold and hard as her toes presently were.

She'd seen enough, but she hesitated. If she could just wait until it got light enough to make out the Navaho's tail numbers. No. It was too risky. She had to get back to the *Avilda* and on board before the men. Already the suitcases were being closed. Stealthily, she rose enough to move in a kind of crouching, sideways walk, hands and feet the only things touching the ground. When she was out of sight she straightened up and ran, no mean feat in a survival suit in the dark, over clumps of rough grass and sudden drifts of snow. Her feet splashed into the water, she fell forward and struck out, suddenly terrified that she would be caught. At first she couldn't see where she was going, then the *Avilda*'s hull swung sharply into focus and with alarm Kate realized how light it was getting. They would see her climbing aboard from shore. Fear spurred her on and she maintained a steady breaststroke, eyes fixed on the *Avilda*'s oh-so-slowly nearing hull, ears straining for the launch of the skiff and the dip of oars in the water.

Her knee hit a rock, probably the same one that got her on

the way in, she thought wearily, and began a halfhearted frog kick. For Harry Gault to have found his way through the series of killer reefs she remembered seeing, he had to have made this trip more than once.

So interesting did she find this thought that she missed her stroke and swallowed a mouthful of seawater and began to choke. A violent cough brought her knees up, a second banged her head against the hull, surprising her into swallowing another lungful of seawater and setting up another bout of hacking. A clumsy hand searched for some kind of hold on the hull, and slid off. God, she was just so tired.

"What the hell?" From a long way off, the voice was young and scared, and a little angry, too. "Kate? Kate, is that you?"

She almost went down for the third time. "Andy?" Then, sharply, "Shh! Sound carries over water. Meet me on the other side."

"What?"

"Hush! The other side of the boat! Meet me around the other side of the boat!"

It took all of her remaining energy to push and pull her way around the hull, ducking beneath the anchor chain at the bow, and by the time she reached the opposite side she was nearly spent. Back on Anua the Navaho revved its engines and began the long whine to takeoff. Galvanized, Kate said, "Andy?"

"I'm here."

She paused for breath, just trying to speak exhausting her all over again. "I can't get up, Andy. Can you help me? Don't turn on the deck lights!"

His whisper was annoyed. "I wasn't going to. Hold on a minute."

"To what?" she asked.

A moment later there was a soft scrape. "Here. Grab this."

It was the boat hook, and with the last ounce of strength left in her Kate grasped at it with both hands, realizing for the first time that she'd forgotten to pull her mittens back on before reentering the water. The suit had been leaking up her arms all the way back to the boat. She wondered in a detached sort of way if her hands had the strength to hold on long enough to get her aboard. The next thing she knew she had collapsed on the deck, gasping like a dying fish. Andy knelt next to her. "Are you all right? What the hell were you doing out there?"

Kate gave a ghost of a laugh. "Surf's up."

"Surf's up, my ass!"

"Why, Andy," she said weakly, "you're sounding more like me every day." A giggle rose to her throat. Recognizing the beginnings of hysteria, she quelled it sternly.

"Where's the skipper? And Ned and Seth?"

Wet, cold, sore, tired, she said, her voice an unconscious plea, "Can you get me to our stateroom?"

In stiff-lipped silence he hauled her to her feet. "No," she said, when he would have taken her through the galley, "let's use the aft cabin door. And you go in first and get some towels so I don't drip all over everything."

He did as she said, helping her out of the survival suit and mopping up the floor where it had dripped. With impersonal hands he stripped her to her skin, rubbed her down and tucked her up in her bunk with three extra blankets on top of her sleeping bag. She was shivering uncontrollably and he wanted to make her a hot drink but she wouldn't let him. "Get into your bunk. Now." When he hesitated, she said, her voice a thin thread of sound, "Now, Andy. Please. They can't know we were awake."

131

He hesitated a little longer, and then reluctantly did as she asked. Together in the darkness, they listened as the bow of the skiff bumped the hull, as oars were shipped, as footsteps padded the length of the boat, as doors creaked open and slid shut.

"Are you asleep?" Andy whispered.

"No," she whispered back.

"Care to tell me what the hell is going on?"

"No," she said. "Not yet."

She went to sleep listening to him toss and turn in the bunk above.

CHAPTER 7

THEY PULLED THE HOOK and got under way early the following morning. Kate slept right through it and woke to a rolling, ocean-going swell and the steady throb of the engines. She yawned and stretched, her muscles sore but not as sore as she'd expected. She heard a muffled noise and looked around. Andy was back under his sheet pyramid, taking up most of their limited floor space. A low hum emanated from beneath it.

"What does that thing do again?" she asked in a lazy voice. "Reinforce your penis?"

"*Prana*. It reinforces my *prana,* and you know it." His fair head poked out from between the sheets. "It's about time you woke up."

"Why? What time is it?"

"High noon."

"Jesus, did I sleep through my watch?" Kate sat up and threw back the sleeping bag.

"Relax. We're going back to Dutch. The skipper's taking us in."

"What!"

"We're going back to Dutch," he repeated, eyeing her with a curious expression.

"The hold isn't even half full," Kate protested. "We haven't picked any pots to speak of, and what we've set are scattered from hell to breakfast up and down the Chain. We're just going to leave them there?"

"Evidently." Andy seemed unperturbed at the prospect, although his paycheck was going to be as short as her own on their return.

She flopped back down on the bunk, her mind busy formulating and discarding scenarios. "Well, well, well. What do you know."

"I don't know. What do *you* know?" He saw her look and said firmly, "I mean it, Kate. What was all that business about last night?"

"Shush!" she hissed.

In a lower voice he demanded, "Where were we? What were the guys doing on shore? What were you doing on shore? What was that plane I heard doing there? Why'd I have to drag you out of the water in a survival suit, and why was it so important that the other guys not see us? What's going on?"

"What did you do with the survival suit?"

"I snuck it back in the locker when no one was in the galley."

She blew out a relieved sigh. "Thanks."

"You're welcome. Now tell me what's going on."

She looked at him, sitting facing her in the middle of the floor, draped in folds of white cloth like some minor Middle Eastern potentate, his legs twisted into an impossible position and a stubborn look on his fresh, open face.

She liked Andy Pence. He was very attractive in his youth and his innocence, and his boundless enthusiasm for all things Alaskan had rekindled her own. She might not have been so open to Olga's tales and teachings had she not been first exposed to Andy's enthusiastic and indiscriminatory endorsement of all things Alaskan. Oh, she would have gone along with the old woman, would have listened to her, might even have taken a few winds with a weaver on a spoke, but it would have been in a mood of amused tolerance and only as a means to an end; specifically, a way to weasel herself into the old woman's confidence. Instead, she had been an actively interested participant. All her childhood she had listened to the stories and watched the ivory carvers and the basket weavers and the *oomingmak* knitters and kayak builders, but she had resisted taking an active part, chiefly, she realized now with no little chagrin, because of her grandmother's determination that she would.

The discovery that Andy's company was a pleasure, New Age enthusiasms and all, was a distinct shock. It was not enough, however, to take him into her confidence. Not yet. "Andy, I'm grateful for what you did last night," she said, meeting his eyes frankly. "I'd about had it. I'm not sure I could have climbed back aboard without help. But I can't tell you what's going on. For one thing, I'm not sure myself. For another, the less you know, the safer you are."

He looked frustrated, and she said, "When it's over, I'll tell you everything you ever wanted to know about Harry Gault and Ned Nordhoff and Seth Skinner but were afraid to ask." She stuck out her hand. "Deal?"

He hesitated. "Promise?"

"Promise."

He took her hand with no enthusiasm. "Okay," he grumbled. "Deal."

"In the meantime, I've got to trust you," she told him. "You've got to keep all this under your hat."

He was hurt. "Of course." He looked at her, a speculative gleam in his clear blue eyes. "You're not really a fisherman, are you?"

She smiled and admitted, "I'm not even a fisherwoman."

"Never mind," he said, consoling her on the mortification she undoubtedly felt at having this disgraceful admission wrung from her. "You're out here now. Even if it is on the *Avilda,* Even if you are working for Harry Gault. And you know, Kate? You are pretty good at it."

"Why, thank you, Andy," she said gravely, and burst out laughing in his affronted face.

• • •

It took the *Avilda* fourteen hours to make her way back to Dutch, and when they tied up at the dock it was too late for Kate to go find Jack. She rose early the following morning and was in the galley assembling breakfast when she heard the thump of feet hitting the deck. The starboard door swung open and she looked up. She recognized him at once. It was the shark who had tried to pick her up in the Shipwreck Bar.

It was obvious that he remembered her, too. He looked her over, an unpleasant grin spreading across his face, and unconsciously her hand took a firmer grip on the knife that was slicing Jimmy Dean's Pure Pork Sausage into neat rounds. "Well now," he said with a geniality as mocking as it was menacing. "Look what we have here." He took a step toward her, and every muscle in her body tightened.

"What the hell do you want?"

Kate closed her mouth and looked around. Harry Gault stood in the passageway, glaring at the shark.

"Why, Harry," the shark said, all his teeth showing,

"I'm just making a neighborly visit." He winked. "How was the fishing last trip?"

"I told you never to come down here," Harry snapped.

The shark looked at Kate. "I can see why," he drawled. "If

only I'd known I'da been after you to share the wealth."

Kate kept her face carefully blank and went back to frying sausage and flipping French toast. The shark strolled over to stand close enough behind her for her to smell his after-shave, which seemed to have been applied with a garden hose.

He sniffed. "Smells good, sweetheart," he said, his voice low, his tone insinuating.

He rubbed up against her back and her eyes narrowed to slits. "I wish I could say the same," she purred.

"You've obviously met," Harry said with awful sarcasm.

The shark heaved a mournful sigh. "At the Shipwreck, week before last. But she ran off with somebody else, didn't you, babe?"

"That so?" Harry said, looking at Kate through narrowed, assessing eyes.

"Yup," the shark said sadly. "Big fucking dude, walks slow, talks slow, but moves pretty goddam fast when it comes to the ladies. Isn't that right, babe?" A hand settled on her waist and prepared to slip down over her hip.

Harry swore. "I told you, Shugak, I warned you, no fucking around on the *Avilda!* You—"

Kate pried the hand loose and turned. "First of all," she told the shark sweetly, "I am not your sweetheart, or your babe. Secondly"—and she looked at Harry Gault with a straight, level gaze—"I told you that your crew was safe from seduction, and they have been. But what I do off this boat is my business, with or without slow-talking, slow-walking men." She turned back to the stove, feeling the gazes of both men fixed on her, one suspicious, the other lascivious, ignoring them both.

The shark didn't like being ignored and was preparing to say so, but Harry growled, "Let's go up to the bridge."

Contriving to squeeze past Kate when there was more than enough room to walk around, the shark followed.

Kate finished cooking breakfast, loaded two plates and climbed the stairs to the bridge. Hearing voices in the chart room and finding the door closed, she kicked it a couple of times. "Skipper? You in there?"

There was a thump, not unlike the hasty closing of a suitcase, followed by whispers and a dragging sound. The door slid open and Harry glared at her.

"I brought up your breakfast." She met his suspicious eyes with an expression as guileless as she could manage, and looked past him at the shark, for whom she still had no name, noticing along the way a rectangular object, just the size— surprise, surprise—of one of those shiny silver metal suitcases photographers use to pack their equipment, covered by a hastily tossed, olive-green army blanket. There must have been a locker hidden somewhere in the chart room. "And a plate for your guest."

The shark grinned, employing every tooth back to and including all four wisdoms. A lesser woman might have felt like Little Red Riding Hood but Kate never had intimidated well. "All this and she can cook, too? Honey, you're the answer to a red-blooded American male's prayer. Harry, old buddy, you've been holding out on me."

Kate set both plates down on the empty chart table, contriving to step on the blanket on the way and expose a corner of the suitcase. Aluminum, shiny, silvery bright. She grinned back at the shark and wrinkled her nose at him. "My name's not honey, either, handsome," she said, and left the room, swaggering, as the shark gave forth with a long, drawn-out howl.

Harry slammed the door closed behind her and her grin

vanished. So that was it. That was the connection. And Ned and Seth were in it up to their ears. No wonder the three of them were so blase about their paychecks. Their paychecks for fishing, that is. It was a safe bet the extracurricular cash they were pulling down more than covered any losses they took from the crab. She returned to the galley and dished up her own breakfast. She was in a hurry to get to Jack but Kate never neglected her stomach.

● ● ●

"The fact that Harry could find his way between all those reefs off Anua, in the dark tells me he didn't just start doing it yesterday."

"What happened to Alcala and Brown?" Jack asked bluntly.

"I don't know," Kate said impatiently. "Don't you see, it doesn't matter. We can use this to nail them. Gault and the rest of them are—"

He interrupted her without apology. "The hell it doesn't matter. They are why you were hired on the *Avilda* in the first place. Their families and the board of Alaska Ventures want to know what happened to them, not to mention two law enforcement agencies and three insurance companies. They don't care about somebody dealing a little dope."

"It wasn't a little dope, it was a lot of dope!"

"Your first priority," Jack said, raising his voice to match hers, "is to discover the circumstances in which Alcala and Brown disappeared and, if possible, to recover their bodies."

"Their bodies are probably in a crab pot at the bottom of the Bering Sea, probably because they stumbled onto this business just like I did. I'm telling you, Jack, these guys are

139

dealing dope wholesale. We got a chance here to cut their connection off at the knees. Get a warrant and search the boat. I'm pretty sure I know where he stashes the stuff, I saw the suitcase in the chart room, so why—"

Again he cut her off. "'Pretty sure' isn't good enough in this case and you know it. You're only a hired gun, Kate, you aren't official. Besides, you know and I know that dope wasn't on the boat thirty minutes after it hit port." He regarded her, not unsympathetically. "Find out what happened to Alcala and Brown," he repeated, "and everything else will fall into line."

"I think I have!"

Jack folded his hands across his stomach with an air of humoring her that Kate wanted badly to puncture. "Prove it," he said simply.

"You mean I have to go back out again?" She remembered that Andy was still a member of the *Avilda*'s crew. With a sinking heart she realized that of course she had to go back out, if not for the reasons Jack was enumerating.

"Yes, you have to go back out again. Probably you're right, probably there was a falling out among thieves, probably this is why they disappeared. But we don't know, and the only people who do are on that boat. Sooner or later, one of them is going to slip, and when they do, you'll be there."

"For how long?" Kate inquired with awful patience.

"As long as it takes." He held up one hand. "And while you're on board they can't take off for Macao."

"Unless they decide to put me with Alcala and Brown," she pointed out.

"There is that," he agreed. "Better be careful."

What the hell happened to Kate's overprotective male watchdog, the one with his testosterone level tattooed on his forehead?

"In the meantime, I'll call in the troops. We'll plant somebody in every bar in this dump and watch for—who'd you say?"

"I call him the shark." She described him, adding, "I don't know his name, Harry didn't introduce us."

"Wonderful. 'The shark.' That ought to narrow it down."

"You saw him," she said defensively. "He was trying to pick me up in the Shipwreck when you found me."

"There wasn't anybody in the Shipwreck that day who wasn't trying to pick you up. The entire Russian Merchant Marine was trying to pick you up. Anyway, you"—he pointed at her—"you get your ass back on the *Avilda* and keep an eye on Gault until we gather enough evidence to return an indictment. I don't want him getting wind of us and disappearing into the doughnut hole. It wouldn't be like it was the first time."

"What do you mean by that?"

"I mean those other names you found. There aren't any men attached to them." He saw her expression and held up a hand. "But wait, there's more. Southeast First Bank is looking for Henderson Gantry. Seems there's a little matter of overdue loan payments, amounting to something like half a million dollars. And they can't find the boats to repossess them." Again Jack forestalled Kate. "It gets better. I had an interesting conversation with the district attorney in San Diego, and they're looking for Harley Gruber. Seems Mr. Gruber subdivided a prime piece of property located, according to the surveyor's marks, somewhere a little to the west of the city, and sold the lots to an Eastern developer for a luxury hotel."

Kate's brow puckered. "Don't strain yourself," Jack said dryly, "to the west of San Diego is the Pacific Ocean. And it's legal. The buyers apparently didn't check beyond Gruber's references, which were above reproach, naturally, since they were forged, and nobody noticed until after the check cleared that the construction crew building this hotel was going to have to be fitted with scuba gear."

Kate grinned in spite of herself. "My, I do like style in a villain."

Jack didn't grin back. "This villain may be a murderer twice over. That we know of." He looked at the bundle of paper in his hand and estimated his chances of producing what he wanted before the turn of the century. They weren't better than fifty-fifty, so he tossed the bundle on the table and quoted from memory. "I tried to trace some of those boats. So far, I know they worked the oil spill, but that's it. Except for one in dry dock in Valdez with a stoved-in hull, they seem to have vanished off the face of the earth. Oh, yes, and another interesting sidebar—the owner listed on the contract with the guy working on repairs is Harold Gunderson." He paused. "I told the guy to stop working, that he probably wasn't going to get paid and that there were probably thirteen claims before his if he filed a lien, but I'm not sure he believed me." Jack shook his head, half in disbelief, half in admiration. "This Gault is some piece of work. When he embezzles, he embezzles down to the last dime. And now you tell me he's wholesaling cocaine."

"He's greedy," she pointed out. "He even shorted us on our crew shares. Not much, a couple hundred each, but he is greedy. Greedy people never get enough. What's coke retail for now? A hundred a gram?"

"More like a hundred twenty-five."

She shrugged. "You see? It's easy money, or it has been so far. How can he resist?"

"I suppose you're right." He paused. "Can you stay for a while?"

She shook her head. "We're not leaving for another six hours, no, but I can't stay."

"Why not? Is Gault on to you? If—"

"No, it's not that. There's somebody I've got to see."

"In Dutch Harbor? What, are the Russians back?"

"You said we need a witness. I might have one for you."

• • •

Twenty minutes brisk walk brought her back to the little clapboard house on the edge of Unalaska village. The lights were on in the kitchen and Kate could see Olga sitting at the table, surrounded by the detritus of basket weaving. She stood still for a moment, watching through the window as the old woman's strong brown fingers attached another spoke with deft movements.

Something in the scene wrung her heart. One woman, old, alone, practicing a craft that had almost died out, that might have had it not been for her. She was the last of her race, and yet there were those six young girls, making their spending money at a skill as old as recorded time. There was something for everyone in the picture, Kate thought, optimist and pessimist alike. A traditionalist might be appalled that basket weaving went on only to fulfill an urgent need for the latest from Run D.M.C., but at least it went on. Andy would approve wholeheartedly.

A movement caught the corner of her eye and she turned her head toward the beach. Sasha sat hunched over at the water's edge, alone, her back to Kate. Kate looked from daughter to mother and back again, and after a brief tussle with her conscience went to squat next to the daughter. When Sasha said nothing, she said, "Hello, Sasha."

Sasha didn't look up. "'Lo, Kate," she said in her slow, thick voice.

"How did you know it was me?"

The hand holding the storyknife didn't pause in its deft, swooping, graceful strokes. "Hear footsteps. Know footsteps. Know you."

Kate smiled a little. "You hear like a fox."

Magically, a fox appeared in front of her in the sand, all ears and tail and pointed, inquiring nose. Sasha looked up and smiled. The smile was crooked, a little unfocused, but the gleam in the brown eyes, half-hidden by drooping lids, was alert and intelligent. "Move like fox. When want."

"I'm sure you do," Kate said, and pointed to a figure off to one side. "More thunderbirds?"

"Thunderbird," Sasha corrected. Both fox and thunderbird disappeared, to be replaced by another thunderbird closer to center stage.

"And kayaks."

"Kayak. Big kayak."

"With men on it," Kate said, watching the tip of the storyknife. "Five men."

Five Y's with legs appeared, to be encompassed with the thunderbird and the kayak inside two concentric circles. "Home."

"Home," Kate repeated. "Where is home, Sasha? Is your island home? Is Anua home?"

"Home," Sasha said firmly, drawing a set of concentric rings, the first just inside the second, to enclose the other figures in two perfect circles. She paused, elbows resting on her knees. A ray of sun gleamed briefly through cloud and fog, shining off the wet sand, throwing the figures drawn there into stark relief. A boat passed by offshore, sending a wavelet to taste the edge of Sasha's drawings.

Kate held her hand out, palm up. "May I try? Please? I've never told a story."

Sasha considered the matter with a thoughtful frown. She must eventually have reached the conclusion Kate was a trustworthy person because she extended her two hands, the storyknife balanced between them like a ceremonial offering. Kate accepted the rich weight of the thing with care. "How do I hold it? Just like a knife? Like this. I see."

"Wipe."

"Wipe?" Kate echoed her teacher. "Oh, I see. Wipe the sand smooth for my story. Okay." With a broad stroke of the blade she swept the sand clear and began to draw. "Thunderbird."

Sasha watched intently. "Longer."

Kate extended the thunderbird's wing. Next to it she drew a crude hull shape. "Kayak."

Sasha made a face. "Everybody's a critic," Kate muttered, and made the three wavy lines beneath the kayak symbol, indicating the ocean. The stick figures were easier, if not as clear or as spirited as Sasha's. "Men come on the kayak." She paused. "Did men come with the thunderbird, too, Sasha?" She made the male figure next to the thunderbird.

"No." Sasha shook her head violently. "No no no no." Snatching for the storyknife, she erased the man figure.

"Oh," Kate said, disappointed but not really surprised. It had been only a guess, after all.

Sasha was drawing in the sand, next to Kate's shaky thunderbird. She drew a male figure. She drew a second. "Mans," she said, sounding like a not very patient schoolteacher trying to impart valuable information to a not very bright student. "Mans."

"Oh," Kate said, light breaking. "Not one man with the thunderbird. Two men with the thunderbird."

"Mans," Sasha repeated, satisfied. She handed back the knife and waited expectantly.

"Okay." Kate hunkered down, shoulder to shoulder with Sasha, both of them absorbed in the drama unfolding in stick figures on the sand before them. "Five men on the kayak, two men with the thunderbird, all home." She paused. "Then what happened?" She balanced the storyknife on her palms and held it out. "What happened after the thunderbird and the kayak came home?"

Slowly, reluctantly, Sasha took the knife and began to draw. It was the man figure again, but twice the size of the others and with eight arms and what looked like horns and fangs and maybe even a tail. "A monster?" Kate guessed.

Sasha looked grave. "Bad. Kill mans."

"The monster killed the men," Kate said, her voice calm although her heart rate had picked up. "All of them? Did the monster kill all the men?"

The storyknife wiped out two of the male figures. "Bad kill mans."

"The monster killed two of the men," Kate agreed. "Did the rest run away?"

Sasha, obviously pleased at this display of intelligence by her backward pupil, gave a firm nod. "Rest run away."

"Sasha," Kate said. "Did the monster kill the men, or did the men kill each other?"

"Bad kill mans," Sasha repeated. "Rest run away."

Kate sat back on her heels and regarded Sasha thoughtfully. "Is home an island, Sasha?" she asked gently. "Is home Anua?"

"Bad kill mans," Sasha said stubbornly. "Rest run away. That's all."

Kate reached for the storyknife again and held it poised, hesitating. There wasn't much point in further questioning. Sasha was no kind of credible witness, and besides, if she had gone home the previous year, she had not gone home alone.

She made as if to sweep the sand smooth once again. "No," Sasha said, gripping her hand and removing the storyknife from it. "Let water take."

Kate relinquished the storyknife with a reluctance she only dimly recognized. The smooth, worn ivory was so warm to the touch, the weight perfectly balanced. It fit so well into her hand. Olga was right. The storyknife was a living thing, with its own spirit. Kate felt privileged to have been permitted to speak through it and she was glad that, as before, she had been judged and not found wanting.

• • •

Kate let herself into Olga's house and walked down the hallway to the kitchen.

The old woman looked up from her weaving and smiled. "Hello, Kate."

"Hello, Auntie."

Olga indicated the table. "Did you come for another lesson?"

Kate sat down. "Why not?"

"I kept your basket for you."

Olga handed it over and Kate eyed it. "This looks like the cat's been chewing on it."

"It's exactly as you left it," Olga said mildly.

"I'm sure it is," Kate said with a sigh.

Olga made tea and put a plate filled with round, golden sugar cookies on the table. The tea was strong and hot and sweet, the cookies crunchy and flavored with lemon. Kate, chilled from the half hour of squatting half in and half out of Iliuliuk Bay and probably still from her swim in the survival suit as well, ate and drank everything she was offered.

Putting her cup down, she said, "I saw Sasha on the beach."

"Oh?"

"Yes. She was drawing with the storyknife. The story about the thunderbird and the kayak and the men."

Olga squinted down at her basket, working out an intricate stitch with intent care.

"This time, she told me about a monster with eight arms. It was bad, she said."

"The *kelet*," Olga said, nodding. "An evil spirit."

"The *kelet*," Kate said, testing the word on her tongue. "Sasha says this *kelet*, this evil spirit, killed two of the men."

"Two of the men?" Olga displayed only polite interest. "This *kelet* must have been very evil indeed. But then they usually are."

"I see." Kate wound a weaver around a spoke. The grass was dry and difficult to work. "She says the other men who came with the thunderbird and the kayak got away."

"In that story, usually the men trick the *kelet* and they all get away. And usually the story says the men are women."

"Sasha and the storyknife say men this time," Kate said cheerfully. She dabbled her fingers in the bowl of water and dampened the weaver. "The last time I was here, didn't you tell me that if you keep picking the rye grass in the same place that the grass gets better?"

"Yes."

Kate paused, wrestling with her weaver. "Did you pick grass in the same spot when you lived on Anua?"

"Yes."

The stitch snugged up against the spoke as if Kate had been weaving all her life, and she viewed it with satisfaction. "And were you picking grass in that same spot in March this year?"

"Whatever would we be doing on Anua in March?" Olga wondered, her expression one of gentle surprise. "The time to pick the grass is in June and July."

"I don't know," Kate admitted. "I haven't figured that out yet."

"Mmm." Olga rose and took the basket from Kate's hands. "You're improving. You should take this with you this time. You can practice on the boat. More tea?"

"Why, yes. Thank you."

They worked together on their baskets. Sasha came in and without speaking settled into a seat next to her mother, plucking a half-made basket from the debris on the table that had a sort of Greek key pattern worked around its base. Her dark hair, carefully trimmed by an inexpert, loving hand, flopped in her face. The tip of her tongue stuck out of one corner of her mouth. She was intent, absorbed, her misshapen fingers as deft at weaving baskets as they were in telling stories in the sand.

Olga broke the silence first. "Have you heard the story of how the first basket was made?"

"I don't think I have." Kate said, bending over her basket again. "I'd like to."

Olga selected another weaver, and when she spoke again her voice had fallen into that singsong kind of near chant that Kate had found so mesmerizing before. It was obvious where Sasha got her talent for telling tales.

"The Sun married the Woman Who Kept the Tides," Olga began.

149

"The Sun's new wife cut the rye grass.

"She cured the grass.

"She split it on her thumbnail.

"She split it into spokes and weavers.

"She made a basket.

"She made it around her husband's thumb.

"When it was finished she took it off his thumb.

"She blew in it.

"It got big.

"She made a rope out of roots.

"She tied the rope to the basket.

"She tied their children to the rope.

"The Sun let the basket go.

"Their children floated down to the world.

"The world was an island.

"It was our island.

"That is how the people came home.

"That's all."

Kate, bent over her basket, inhaled the top of a slender frond of split grass and sneezed violently. "Sorry. So which island did the people come to, Auntie?"

"Anua, of course." Olga laughed, a rich, merry laugh. Sasha laughed, too, less richly, less merrily. "On every island, in every village, it is the same. The legend may be different, but the old ones tell the children it was *their* island the children of the Sun and the Woman Who Kept the Tides came to. *Their* island is always the first island, and it is from *their* island that all Aleuts come."

Kate grinned. "I have heard that story before, Auntie. Only it was the children of the Daughter of Calm Waters and Agudar, the Moon, Master Spirit and Keeper of the Game, and the way my grandmother told it, the people floated down to Atka."

Olga laughed again, and again Sasha echoed the sound. "You see? Every island tries to be the best." She held up her basket. "In weaving. In storytelling. In everything."

Maybe even in guile, Kate thought.

She took her leave soon afterward, carrying with her the few rounds she had woven into a gnawed-looking little base, a small sheaf of spokes and weavers, and the certainty that if the need arose, she wouldn't have a witness to the events that took place on Anua Island the previous March.

She had all of the story now, though, or all of the most important parts. She could have pushed for a more definite description, but she didn't have to, and she wouldn't, and Olga knew she wouldn't. There was a bond between them, a link in a chain that went back a thousand generations. At one level of that chain there was race, white against brown. On another level was the ingrained, innate, inherent respect every Aleut has for their elders. The elders were the wise ones, the teachers, for many generations all the law and history there was among the people. With all Olga's authority of eighty winters, Kate couldn't, she simply could not interrogate her. She was too young, Olga was too old, she knew too little, Olga too much.

On a third level, and perhaps the strongest level of all, they shared the unspoken but very real determination to see that Sasha took no harm. She would not be uprooted from everything that was familiar to her to be hammered away at by some Anglos anxious to bring people she didn't know to justice for killing other people she didn't know, Anglos who would be both impatient of and repulsed by her disability.

No. She would remain instead on the beach of her birth,

wielding her storyknife in the gray sand, telling stories to a rapt, enchanted audience of Unalaska girls for generations to come.

The thought pleased Kate, and she quickened her pace over the Bridge to the Other Side. She hoped young Andy hadn't managed to stir up any trouble in her absence. That boy needed a keeper.

CHAPTER 8

KATE'S FEET HIT the deck with a satisfying thump. Crossing over had not been such an ordeal this time, as it was still light out and this time the *Avilda,* bless her heart, was only the second boat out from the dock. Whistling, she opened the door to the galley. The whistle died on her lips.

The whole crew was there. Harry Gault, standing, had his arms crossed across his chest and a glower on his face, but as that was his natural expression Kate ignored it. Ned looked as if he might take a bite out of the next person to walk too close to him, but that, too, was natural. Seth, as usual, looked tranquil, even a little bored. Andy was wide-eyed and apprehensive and looked every one of his nineteen years.

The Coast Guard was there, too, in the persons of two officers, crisp and official in blue uniforms, clipboards held at shoulder arms. One was short and stocky and white-haired, the other was short and skinny with brown hair that curled out from beneath his cap in an undisciplined mass. Her cap, Kate realized. When the door opened they turned.

"Hi," she said, shutting the door behind her. "Don't mind me, I'm just the other deckhand."

She leaned up against the wall next to the door and shoved her hands in her pockets. She knew immediately what was going on. It was a snap safety inspection. What with federal cutbacks they didn't happen all that often anymore, but neither were they unknown, the proof positive standing four feet away from her. She was only sorry that engine maintenance didn't come within the Coasties' purview. She settled back and prepared to enjoy herself.

"Your mast light is out, your fire extinguishers needed servicing six months ago, your EPIRB hasn't been tested in seven months, you've forgotten the last time you assembled the crew for an emergency drill, and you can't find your ship's log to jog your memory," the older Coastie said. "Pretty sloppy seamanship, Captain Gault. It's going to cost you."

The thin officer stared around her with a puzzled air. "This is the *Avilda,* isn't it?"

Harry ignored her and Ned only scowled. Andy looked as if his vocal cords had frozen in place and Kate wouldn't have volunteered a helpful remark if her life depended on it. "Yes," Seth said laconically.

"Owned by Alaska Ventures? Out of Freetown, Oregon?" Seth nodded.

The officer looked back down at her list. "I'd never have believed it."

"Okay," the first officer said, "flotation devices."

"There's a survival suit for every crewman on board," Harry Gault growled.

"Standard procedure on any boat owned by Alaska Ventures," the second officer said, and met Harry's glare with a smile that said she hoped Harry might try to make something out of the implied insult. Kate found herself liking the younger Coastie without any effort at all.

"Well, trot 'em out," the first officer said impatiently. "Come on, your survival suits. Let's see 'em."

Kate was suddenly very still. Her eyes met Andy's across the galley, his alarmed, hers holding a distinct warning.

Nobody moved. Again, it was Seth who broke the stalemate

by coming forward and pulling up the seat of the bench that ran around the galley table. He stood staring down for a moment.

"Well?" the first officer said impatiently. "Haul 'em out, let's take a look."

"Okay," Seth said equably, "but one of 'em you won't have to check. It's already been used."

Harry's head snapped around. "What?"

In reply, Seth reached into the locker and produced the survival suit that Kate had field-tested two nights before. It wasn't exactly dripping, but it had been folded and put away wet. Some of the folds still held water. As they watched, a drop of seawater collected in one fold and dripped to the floor.

The galley was very still. Slowly, Harry looked up, first at Andy, and then, a much longer and more considering look, at Kate. She met his eyes with a slight lift of her brows. The silence stretched out. "What?" she said, ignoring the wet survival suit dangling from Seth's hand, staring straight at Harry with as much innocence as she could muster. "What's the problem?"

Oblivious, the thin officer was pawing through the locker. "One, two, three, four," she said. "And five." She looked up and counted heads. "One, two, three, four, five. All but four in the original, unopened packaging."

The stout officer scratched his head. "You know we can't require you to test those suits. Hell, it was only recently we were allowed to require you to carry them. But," he said, bending a hard look on the skipper, "you have got to know that it's a whole lot safer when your crew is versed in survival suit operations. Look what happened to the *Daisy Mae*. We found a survival suit still in its package. Hadn't even been opened. Hadn't even been tried on." He gestured. "Not like this one. Ought to have let it dry out before you put it back, though."

"I guess I better 'fess up," Andy said suddenly. Everyone turned toward him, as, behind them, Kate shook her head violently. Ignoring her, he said, "I got curious and tried it on this morning. And then I thought what the hell and took a little dip in the harbor." He grinned. "I'm from Ventura. I'm used to surfing every day. I miss the water."

The two officers exchanged a wooden glance. "There's a world of difference between the water off Ventura and the water in Iliuliuk Bay," the stocky officer said dryly. "The idea here is to keep the hell out of the water if at all possible." He looked back at his clipboard, making a minute notation to his list. "Anyway, the point is to maintain your boat in such a fashion that you don't have to go swimming." He ripped off a copy and held it out to Harry. For a moment Kate thought he wasn't going to take it. Seth nudged him, and he extended a reluctant hand.

The slip was thrust into it unhesitatingly. "Your owners will receive formal notice within ten days to two weeks. If I were you, I'd see to rectifying those violations before you ship out again. And if your mooring light is gone, maybe you should check your stock of bulbs for running lights. They generally tend to need to be replaced all at the same time." He touched the brim of his cap. "Good-bye." Like a skinny mirror image, the second officer echoed the movement. "It's been swell," Kate heard her breathe, and then they were gone.

• • •

Harry chewed Andy out for a good five minutes, using every

four-letter word in the book and some he made up on the spot, and when he was done, Ned took over. When he was finished, Andy looked, if not squelched, at least a trifle subdued. Kate stood in the galley with him, knowing he had taken the onus of suspicion on himself, angry because he had, a little grateful, too, and more than a little touched by the gesture. She only hoped it didn't get him killed.

She had no chance to express any of these feelings. Ned took the first watch and they rumbled out of the harbor on the evening tide. It was too early to go to bed, and Kate thought it best to fall in with the first night out's regular routine. There was some discussion as to who and what would occupy the VCR in the rec room. Seth chose *Debbie Does Dallas,* as expected, Andy chose *Gandhi,* also expected, and Harry chose *The Dam Busters,* which show of good taste amazed Kate. The fact that the movie was even in Harry's library amazed her even more, before she realized that their selection was probably standard issue on Alaska Ventures's boats. Kate, who harbored a secret letch for John Wayne, chose *Rio Lobo.* "Who wants popcorn?"

"Me!" came a chorus of three.

"Butter?"

"Lots!"

John Wayne saved the Union in spite of itself one more time and Andy got up to rewind the tape and start *Gandhi.*

"Did you know," Seth said.

Kate, full of buttered popcorn and relief, said lazily, "What?"

"Did you know that the last shot fired in the Civil War was fired around these parts?"

"What," Kate said, "you mean around these here Aleutian parts?"

"Uh-huh."

"No way," she said.

"Come on," Andy said.

"Bullshit," Harry agreed.

"It's true. The summer of 1865, the Confederate Navy ship *Shenandoah* blew almost forty Union ships out of the Bering Sea. Whalers, merchant vessels, anything flying the wrong flag. On June 26 Waddell—he was the skipper—took six whalers off St. Lawrence Island alone. Two days later he took eleven more in the Bering Strait. See, the Confederacy was trying to hit the Yankees in the wallet."

"Wait a minute," Kate said, who wasn't a John Wayne fan for nothing, "Lee surrendered in April."

"The *Shenandoah* was umpteen thousand miles from home in April," Seth said, "and they couldn't afford a satellite dish. They didn't know. What's more, they were never caught. When a British ship told them the war was over, Waddell sailed her all the way around the Horn and back to England, where he surrendered to the American ambassador."

"Wow!" Andy said, eyes shining. "So the last shot of the Civil War was fired off the coast of Alaska! That's great! Isn't that great, Kate?"

Still suspicious, Kate said, "How come I've never heard of this before?"

"Why, I don't know, Kate," Seth said, so mildly it was impossible to suspect him of malice. "Could it be that you don't know everything after all?"

"I never said I did," Kate said, hurt, and made an instantaneous resolve upon next setting foot on shore to find the nearest history of the Civil War and look it up.

The credits for *Gandhi* rolled. Seth yawned and mumbled something about a long day. Harry was right behind him.

Kate, who liked Ben Kingsley almost as much as she liked John Wayne, and who had no TV or VCR in her little cabin in the middle of a million square acres of federal park and so didn't get to see movies unless she was visiting Bobby, stayed put. She would have stayed put for *Debbie Does Dallas*.

When the door closed behind Harry she waited a few moments before saying in a low voice, "Andy? Thanks."

He flushed up to the roots of his hair. Trying for nonchalance, his voice squeaked, and he flushed again. He cleared his throat and said gruffly, "Forget it." He picked up the remote and pretended to fiddle with the tracking. "You ever going to tell me what you were doing on that island? Or what they were doing there?"

"Sometime."

"But not now?"

She shook her head. "Andy?" He looked at her and sobered at her expression. "This is my last trip on the *Avilda*. It should be yours, too."

"I haven't found another berth yet, I—"

"I'll help you find one," she said. "Let's get off the *Avilda* while we can still walk off. Okay?"

The color left his face, leaving it pale beneath his fading tan. "Okay."

They settled back to watch the movie. When it was over, Andy said on a long sigh, "Now there's a man who is on the road to Enlightenment."

Kate hid a grin. "No need to reinforce his *prana*, I guess."

"No, Kate," Andy said earnestly, "everyone has to do that. 'You must perform thy allotted work, for action is superior to inaction.' Like Jesus, Gandhi preached love of your fellow man, and he performed his allotted work so well that his legacy was a free India."

"And look how well things turned out there," Kate told him. "Pakistan and India are at each other's throats, they're starving in Bangladesh, Sri Lanka is in the middle of a civil war and every two or three years the Muslims murder a hundred or so Hindus, or the other way around. Some legacy, all right."

"'Always perform the work that has to be done without attachment,'" Andy quoted solemnly, "'for man attains the Supreme by performing work without attachment.'"

"Is there anything you don't believe in?" she demanded, exasperated. "There's got to be some crackpot religion you've overlooked. Zoroastrianism? The Cathars? Have you accidentally let a recruiter for the Rosicrucian Fellowship pass you by?"

"'The ignorant man who is without faith and of a doubting nature perishes.'" And the little prick had the nerve to grin at her.

CHAPTER 9

THE NEXT DAY WAS as balmy as it got in the Aleutians. It wasn't raining, snowing or sleeting, the omnipresent bank of fog stayed low on the southeastern horizon, and there were enough breaks in the clouds overhead for the sun to peep through occasionally with at least the illusion of warmth and cheer. A strong, regular swell caused the deck of the *Avilda* to lift and fall rhythmically beneath their feet but there was no breaking spray, and except where their hands got wet on the lines they worked dry for the first time in anyone's memory. Kate found that she was actually enjoying herself.

She was hanging a bait jar when she heard Andy cry out. She wormed her head and shoulders out of the pot and stood. "What?"

His eyes blazing with excitement, he pointed to port. "Look! Look at them all!"

It was a pod of killer whales, cresting and blowing, their backs gleaming black and white in the erratic sun.

"For a minute I thought they were sharks," Andy said.

There was awe in his voice and Kate smiled to herself.

"Why are they called killer whales?"

"Because they do."

"What, kill? I thought whales only ate krill."

Kate's hands paused as she looked over at him. "And what do you know about krill?"

"Hey, I went to college." He was tying door ties with a deftness that had not been present a month, even two weeks before. "For one semester, anyway. I took a class in marine biology when I knew I was coming to Alaska."

"And you didn't learn about killer whales?"

"Well, I kind of… left… before we got to killer whales." He gave her an engaging grin. "So. What do killer whales kill?"

"Actually, they aren't whales, they're the largest dolphin. And they eat just about anything they can fit into their mouths," Kate replied, loading bait jars. Even the smell of dead herring wasn't as bad this morning. "Seals, mostly, but any kind of fish, squid, penguins, sea lions. Even other whales." She screwed down the lid on one jar. "They've even been known to attack boats."

"Wow," Andy breathed. "You mean like *Moby Dick*?"

Kate nodded, and he stared at the retreating backs of the orcas, upright fins slicing through the water. "They're probably hunting now," Kate added. "They hunt in pods." Olga's chant flashed through her mind. *"When the killer whales come to a bay with a village, someone dies in that bay."* A whisper of unease crept up her spine. She shrugged it off and said to Andy, "Did I ever tell you I used to sing high sea chanteys?"

He was unable to repress an expression of alarm. "No."

"Well, I did." She whacked vigorously at a block of frozen herring. "There was a song the whalers used to sing on their way south." And for the first time in two years she raised her voice in song. It was harsh, grating across the wound in her throat and coming out low and raspy, but it seemed somehow appropriate to the place and the day and the killer whales frolicking with lethal intent off their port bow.

"'Tis a damn tough life full of toil and strife
We whalemen undergo

162

And we don't give a damn when the gale is done
How hard the winds did blow."

She grinned at Andy, who looked like he was falling in love.

"Now we're homeward bound 'tis a grand old
sound
On a good ship taut and free,
And we won't give a damn when we drink our
rum
With the girls of old Maui."

She handed Seth a full bait jar so he could hang it in the pot about to go over the side. He took it and didn't immediately turn to hang it, but stood for a moment, looking down at her. Her smile faded. "What's the matter?"

He shrugged. "Nothing," he said, and turned back to the shot of line he was coiling.

She stared at his back, puzzled. The expression in his eyes had seemed somehow regretful. She shrugged and went back to the bait table to cut more herring and fill more jars.

"Rolling down to old Maui, my boys,
Rolling down to old Maui
Now we're homeward bound from the Arctic
round
Rolling down to old Maui."

She couldn't remember the last time she'd felt this good. Her last trip on the *Avilda*, and no matter what Jack said it was going to be her last trip, was going to be a piece of cake.

163

As soon as they nailed the shark in Dutch, he'd put them on to the men in the Navaho, and when they finished singing, the truth of what had happened to Alcala and Brown would be known at last. Harry Gault had no real idea there was a cuckoo in his nest, and all Kate had to do was help set and pull pots and make money and count the knots home. She hoped Jack had remembered to make her a reservation on the plane. The flights north were always jammed and she wanted to be on the first one that left after her tippy toe hit dirt at Dutch. She missed Mutt and her cabin and her homestead and the Park, though it didn't look like she was going to miss the first snow after all.

> "How soft the breeze from the island trees
> Now the ice is far astern
> And them native maids in them tropical glades
> Is awaiting our return."

She was able to dismiss Harry catching her coming out of his cabin at two in the morning; he hadn't so much as raised an eyebrow in her direction, or referred to it in any way. He had likewise ignored her reference to his two previous crewmen's disappearance, probably having decided she'd heard the story over a bar in Dutch. He hadn't picked up on the shark's reference to Jack, and Andy, bless his heart, had covered for the wet survival suit.

> "Even now their big black eyes look out
> Hoping some fine day to see—
> Our baggy sails running 'fore the gales
> Rolling down to old Maui."

She leaned head and shoulders inside a crab pot balanced delicately on the pot launcher, and began to hang the bait jar. Through the metal mesh stretched between the steel frames, she saw Ned raise his right hand, as if to wave toward the bridge. His left hand moved to the launching lever.

The engine changed pitch, the *Avilda* made a sudden jerk to port and the platform of the pot launcher shifted. The pot tilted precariously, overbalanced and fell into the water.

It wasn't until Kate inhaled water and exhaled bubbles that she realized she had fallen with it.

Her first thought was how strange it was that her mind never stopped thinking, that she remained unpanicked, that she could assess her situation so coolly, ticking off items one at a time.

She realized she was overboard.

She realized she was inside a crab pot.

She realized it was no accident, and dismissed the knowledge as something to be dealt with later.

She spared one brief, bitter thought for the cocksure arrogance that led her to believe she was safe. No, safe wasn't the right word. She had thought herself invulnerable. That, too, was something better dealt with later.

Meanwhile, she and the pot were sinking together, down, down, down, heading straight down through the cold, green waters of the Gulf of Alaska, water that grew ever darker as they descended toward the ocean bottom three hundred feet below.

Kate realized the killers had had no time to tie the door shut before dumping the pot. It had happened so fast, she still had the strap of the jar hanger in one hand. Instinctively, she used it to brace herself and kicked at the door. It didn't move. She kicked again. It remained closed, perhaps the force of their descent causing the water to keep it closed, perhaps the water blunting the force of her kicks.

The pressure of all that water bearing down on her pitifully fragile self was building in her ears.

It would kill her.

If hypothermia didn't get her first.

If she didn't drown before that.

She kicked again, and still that damn door wouldn't budge, and suddenly she was overwhelmed with an energizing, revitalizing fury and she kicked again and again and again. She would not be disposed of like an inconvenience, Harry Gault and Seth Skinner and Ned Nordhoff would *not* be permitted to go their way as if nothing had happened, business as usual, she *would* get out of this pot, she *would* fight her way to the surface, she *would* flay all three of them alive and shove *them* over the side in a crab pot and see how *they* liked it.

She kicked again and her foot hit nothing. The fury cleared from her eyes and she saw that the door to the crab pot was open, forced by the water all the way open and back against the side of the pot. Without hesitation she grabbed mesh to the open end and, because the pot had tumbled and was descending door side down, pulled herself around the bottom and up the other side, virtually climbing around the outside of the pot.

When she reached the top she hesitated for a millisecond. As rapidly as it was descending toward the ocean bottom, as much as the pressure was building in her ears, as numb as her hands and feet were becoming, still the pot was the only solid object in her world at that moment, and it took a conscious effort to let go and strike for the surface.

She did it, though, following the long trail of bubbles up, upward, ever upward, stroking vigorously with arms that felt like lead, kicking steadily with legs that felt like spaghetti. Her lungs began to burn from lack of oxygen. Was she still going up? Had she become disoriented and lost her sense of direction? Was she already drowned and didn't know it? The temptation to inhale, to gulp in great breaths of air, was so tempting that she opened her mouth to do just that when she saw a dark shape above her.

It was the hull of the *Avilda*, and with a burst of adrenaline she reached out for it with every numb sinew of her body. As it came nearer some detached corner of her mind noticed that the keel had enough kelp growing from it to qualify as a sea otter habitat. It must have slowed the *Avilda*'s cruising speed by at least five knots. But then, what could you expect from a skipper whose creed was "Use it up, throw it out and buy a new one"?

The thought of Harry Gault, laughing at how he'd tricked her, triumphant in his successful disposal of what was surely nothing more than a temporary annoyance, less in importance than a rock he would stub his toe on, cleared Kate's head at once. She was close enough to where she could see the surface through the water now, could even make out the clouds in the sky. She made for the side of the boat, hoping to attract Andy's attention, but the side kept retreating in front of her. Her lungs bursting and her ears popping, she made for the surface, breaking out of the sea's cold embrace into air that felt even colder.

Gasping for breath, coughing water out of her lungs, she shook water from her eyes and looked up.

Just in time to see the stern of the *Avilda* swing toward her, the water boiling out from beneath its stern. Instinct took over and she sucked in and dived straight down as far and as fast as she could.

Even at that, the churning propellor tickled one booted foot. Another stroke and she was beyond it, just barely.

A flood of incredulous wrath filled her entire body, driving out cold, cramp and lack of air, although later she wondered why incredulous. Harry Gault had seen her surface. Harry Gault had seen her, had realized she had fought her way out of the pot and back to the surface, and had swung the stern of the *Avilda* around to try to catch her in the propellor and finish the job once and for all.

Furiously calm, letting the air stored in her lungs out one minuscule bubble at a time, she let herself drift for a moment, studying the movement of the hull above her. She could see it quite clearly, and the propellor, as well as the rudder, and she waited, sure of Harry's next move. When the rudder shifted to starboard she struck for the port side of the vessel and broke surface just as the aft cabin was slipping by. Something wet and slimy trailed across her cheek and with a reflexive motion she reached up to claw it away.

It was the lady's line.

The lady's line, the line Ned threw over the side when they were done fishing and ready to head for home. The thought that he had felt confident enough that the day's business was done to throw the line overboard banished the fear that her hands might be too numb to grip, and she forced her fingers around the rope.

On her peripheral vision she thought she saw the flash of a triangular fin, a white patch on a shiny black back, and for the first time she was truly afraid. That fear was enough to propel her up the rope, hand over hand, breaking the surface, bringing her feet down against the hull, walking up it, braced back against the pull of the lady's line. She caught at the railing with one hand, dropped the line and grabbed with the other. Scrabbling with her toes, she threw a leg over the railing and pulled herself up and over it, to collapse on the deck and lie there soaked and shaking in a puddle of seawater.

Never had air tasted sweeter, never had the deck of the *Avilda* felt firmer, never had she felt so alive. Life was good.

"When killer whales come to a bay with a village, someone dies in that village," she muttered, half hysterically. "But not this time, Auntie. Not today. Not me."

Yes, life was good. If she wanted it to stay that way she had to move. She rolled over and came to her knees and banged at the sides of her head, shaking water from her ears. Raised voices came to her from the foredeck, and crouching, her back pressed up against the cabin, she inched her way forward. Where the side of the cabin began to curve into the front, she stopped to listen.

"That's all you're going to do?" she heard Andy say, his young voice agonized. "We've got to look for her. We've got to at least try!"

"Forget it, kid," Ned's voice growled back. "She's gone. There's no buoy we can hook on to. That pot wasn't attached to a shot yet anyway."

"Seth?"

"Forget it, kid." Seth's voice was just as gruff but kinder. "It happens. Let's just get back into port."

Andy said no more. Kate, peering cautiously around the corner, saw him with tears coursing down his face, and wondered how she could attract his attention without attracting the attention of everyone else and without it being such a wonderful surprise to have his darling Kate back that he gave her away. If only he weren't so young. If only Jack were on board in his place. But if Jack had been on board she would have brained him with her Louisville ice breaker long ago.

She drew back and hoisted a cautious eye over the edge of the porthole in the galley door. It was empty. Swiftly, silently, she opened it and slipped inside. The warmth hit her like a blow and she staggered beneath it. She steadied herself and made for the passageway. A movement caught the corner of her eye and she saw Seth gaping at her through the opposite door.

"Shit!" She dived through the entry into the passageway, hearing the starboard side door to the galley bang open and thumping footsteps behind her. She ran past the doors leading to the staterooms and out the door that led to the aft deck. She launched herself down the stairs and into the storeroom. She cast about desperately for some kind of defense among the stacked cases of canned goods, the burlap sacks of onions and potatoes, the industrial-size refrigerator and the hated walk-in freezer. There was nothing, not so much as a butcher knife or an AK-47. She had time for one longing thought of the baseball bat stacked next to the sledgehammers in the fo'c'sle before she heard a footstep on the stairs. Fear at being caught unprepared sharpened her wits, and she improvised.

He came down the stairs slowly, one cautious foot at a time. Somewhere during the chase he'd picked up a very large monkey wrench and he was carrying it ready to swing. Any liking Kate Shugak had felt for Seth Skinner vanished in that moment.

"Kate?" he said in a low voice. "Come on out. Come on, you know there's no place to go. Don't make this any harder than it has to be."

She crouched behind the Elberta Freestone Peach Halves in Light Syrup, not moving.

The footsteps halted on the other side of her canned goods revetment. Her heart was banging so loudly in her ears she was afraid he could hear it. A drop of seawater, mixed with sweat, gathered on her forehead and rolled down her nose to splash onto the floor, and to Kate the 1964 earthquake and tidal wave combined had made less noise.

"Kate," Seth said sternly, sounding for all the world like a strict, no-nonsense father chastising a recalcitrant child, "I know you're in the freezer, you left the door open. Come on out now."

By then Kate was so conditioned to failure she almost got up. His voice stilled her.

"You've just come out of the water. You must be freezing in there, literally. Come on out. The game's over. Hey, I haven't even told the rest of them you're back on board. It's just me here. Come on."

The creak of the freezer door sounded loud and joyously in Kate's ears and she tensed in every muscle of her quivering body. She heard him take one step, another, and with every ounce of strength she possessed hurled herself forward, knocking the boxes into him and him into the freezer.

There was a yell and a flash of light; he'd been reaching for the string that dangled from the single bulb in the middle of the freezer just as she'd hit him from behind and had pulled it on his way down. She didn't stop to question her good fortune, she kicked boxes out of the way of the door while he was scrambling to his feet and slammed the door shut in his face.

The latch clicked and Kate banged the locking bar down into its bracket with a feral cry. The thud of his body against the door one second too late made it vibrate beneath her cheek. She heard yells and curses and after a moment he began to bang on the door with the monkey wrench. The noise was muffled by the sound of the engine and by the thickness of the door itself, but she leaned up against the door anyway, ear pressed against it, trembling from cold and relief and elation, drinking in the sounds.

Straightening, she turned toward the stairs. One down. Two to go. She wondered if he'd been telling the truth. She hadn't heard him yell out when he'd seen her. If he'd been lying, Andy—she couldn't think about Andy now.

The passageway was still and silent, and she mounted the stairs. The beat of the engine through the walls of the engine room didn't falter. It was warm and dark in the stairwell, and the beat of the engine was hypnotic, a steady chant enticing her to rest, to sit down and relax for just a second. She tried and failed to remember what relaxing felt like, and shied away from the seductive temptation to sit down and find out. She opened the door to the deck. Her teeth were beginning to chatter and she was reluctant to leave the cozy stairwell for the cold, open air.

Her reluctance abated when she realized she'd forgotten the boat hook racked next to that door, as well as the ladder leading to the catwalk, the catwalk that circled all the way around the cabin's second story to the bridge itself. The bridge where Harry Gault stood before a large, spoked wooden wheel, steering his ship into harbor, no doubt smug as all get out in his sense of self-satisfaction over a difficult job well done.

She was about to mount the ladder when a gasp startled her. She jerked around, boat hook at the ready.

Andy was standing there, blue eyes enormous in his white face. "Kate?" He took one faltering step forward. "Kate! You're alive!"

She let go the ladder and leapt forward to slap one hand over his mouth. "Shut up!"

Ignoring her, he folded her in his arms and hugged her

unselfconsciously, his head buried in her soaking hair, muttering over and over again, "Thank God, thank God, thank God. I thought you were drowned. We all did. Thank God you weren't! How did you get back on board? *When* did you get back on board? Why didn't you—"

"Andy," she said, shaking him, "hush up. Dammit, I said be *quiet!*"

Her hissed words finally penetrated his consciousness and he pulled back to stare down at her, his expression confused.

"Never mind how, but my going overboard was no accident."

He stared down at her, his hands lax on her arms.

"It's true, dammit!" she said fiercely, her teeth beginning to chatter again. "N-Ned signaled t-to H-Harry to throw the b-boat on a sh-sharp tack wh-while h-he l-launched the pot. Th-they w-waited until I was h-hanging the b-bait jar."

"Why?" he said simply.

"Th-they're sm-smuggling dope." His face changed. "C-cocaine. Th-they land it on A-Anua and s-sell it in D-Dutch."

His face changed again, to something older and harder. Looking at her through narrowed eyes, he said, "What are you, really? A cop?"

She was surprised at his quickness, and immediately ashamed of her surprise. She wouldn't have liked him so much if he was just another dumb blond. "N-no." She took a deep, shuddering breath, trying to control the shudders rippling through her body. "N-never mind that now. Seth's locked in the meat freezer in the storeroom."

"What!"

"But there's still Ned and Harry. I don't think they know I'm back on board yet. I want you to lock yourself in our stateroom and stay there until I come to get you."

He stared at her. "Lock myself in our room?" He drew himself up, seeming to grow a foot and age twenty years in a single instant. When he spoke his voice was deep and certain. "I won't go to my stateroom like a good little boy, Kate. I'm not a good little boy."

"Keep your voice down!" She had pulled him against the bulkhead of the aft cabin and they crouched there together, speaking in furious whispers.

"I want to help," he said, his face stubborn.

"You want to what?"

He gave the pale imitation of a grin, but it was a grin nevertheless. "'Not by abstention from actions does a man gain freedom, and not by mere renunciation does he attain perfection.' Lead on, MacDuff."

She swore once, and gave in. "Is Harry on the bridge?"

"He was the last time I looked."

"Where's Ned?"

"Picking up the deck."

"Okay. I'm taking this boat hook up the ladder after Harry. Can you distract Ned long enough for me to do it? Then the two of us can take him on."

The scared look was back but he said stoutly, "No problem." He rose to his feet.

"Andy!" He paused in the act of turning the corner of the cabin and looked back at her inquiringly. "Be careful, dammit. No heroics, no trying to take him yourself. These guys are playing for keeps. They've already killed twice. Once they find out you're in the know, they'll try to kill you, too."

His grin flashed and a measure of his youthful cockiness returned. "I love you, too, Kate. Even if you are a heathen and an atheist." He disappeared around the corner of the cabin before her tired mind could formulate a retort. A moment later she heard his voice. "Hey, Ned. Something in the fo'c'sle I think you should see."

Kate could hear the bad temper in Ned's responding growl.

"No," Andy said, far too cheerfully to still be mourning Kate, "this I think you've got to see for yourself."

"It's show time," Kate muttered. "Move your ass, Shugak." As Ned was so fond of saying. She went up the ladder and slithered onto the catwalk. There was only the catwalk beneath her and the bulkhead of the cabin's second story on her right; the rest was open sky, and Kate had never felt so exposed or so vulnerable. Every time the *Avilda* creaked, every time the boat hook scraped against something, every time her wet clothing caught on something else and she had to pull it free, she started and froze in place and had to talk herself forward. After about a year of this she reached the portside door of the bridge.

She didn't stop to think or plan or calculate the odds; she was too far gone for that. In one smooth motion she swung the door open and, boat hook held in a loose grip in both hands in front of her, darted inside.

The bridge was empty.

So was the chart room.

She dropped like a stone to the floor of the bridge and swore helplessly and uselessly. "God *damn* it."

She propelled herself crablike through the opposite door and back out onto the catwalk, where she crouched, flattened up against the bulkhead and tried to think of what the hell to do next.

There was a yell from the forward deck and her head snapped around, straining anxiously to see what had happened.

The worst possible sight met her eyes. Andy in one hand, the baseball bat in the other, Ned emerged from the fo'c'sle door. Andy's face was bleeding profusely and one of his arms was bent up behind his back in a remorseless grip whose force showed clearly on his agonized face. "Harry! I got the kid! Get the bitch!"

There was a shout aft in reply, followed by the sudden pounding of rapidly moving feet. Kate took one last look at Andy's bruised and battered face and gathered herself to tackle Harry as he went by beneath her.

A miracle occurred. Ned, attention divided between hanging on to Andy and calling for backup, tripped over the raised edge of the hold and lost his balance. He dropped the bat, which clattered down to the deck and rolled out of reach. He dropped Andy, who fell to his hands and knees, his head hanging, blood dripping from it to the deck. Ned waved his arms to catch his balance. It didn't work. The hatch cover, which Andy had apparently caught Ned in the act of replacing over the hold when Andy called him to the fo'c'sle, lay over only one corner of the opening.

Into the hold Ned went, headfirst, in a swan dive that would have earned him ten points in any Olympic competition. The hold was only half full, but it was only half full of salt water and tanner crab, and he disappeared beneath a scrabbling layer of long, spiny legs and claws. His head reappeared immediately, spitting, coughing, his arms reaching frantically for purchase that wasn't there. "Help! Harry! Help me! Harry!"

Kate surged to her feet. "Andy! *Andy!* Close the hold! *Close the hold!*"

Andy, still on his hands and knees, shook his head, once, twice, and just as Kate, despairing, had decided he was too dazed to hear her or understand what she was saying, he crawled forward. He laid hands on the hatch cover, a metal lid six feet square that probably weighed more than he did. Kate could hear him grunting from where she crouched. He was a fearful sight, his face twisted into a snarl of strain, covered in congealing blood. For one awful second that seemed to last a year the hatch cover resisted, and then the *Avilda,* as if she knew, took a steep slide down an unexpected swell, Newton kicked in and the hatch cover slid over the hold with a resounding clang.

As the last light disappeared Ned's voice rose to a shriek, until the *Avilda*'s hull seemed to vibrate from the sound. "Harry! Ouch shit get away from me goddam motherfucking sonofabitch I'll kill you you cocksucking little bastard HARRY GET ME OUT OF HERE!"

Unhearing, uncaring, Andy collapsed forward on the hatch cover and lay there. The running footsteps had ceased at Ned's first yell for help but the slide of wet leather against a slippery deck alerted Kate. She tore her attention from the forward deck and peered cautiously over the catwalk. Harry was crouched against the railing, a pistol in his hand, sighting carefully around the corner of the cabin. Terrified, Kate grabbed instinctively for the boat hook with both hands and thrust it hook first over the side of the catwalk.

Just when she could have used a nice gale-force breeze to make some covering noise in the rigging, the wind died. She must have made some sound, because Gault whipped around and looked up, in the same motion raising the gun. There was a loud *bang*, a smack and a whine of a bullet hitting and ricocheting off metal, Gault's savage curse, another shot and another as Kate crouched back out of range. She thought of Andy, all smiles and ideals, all energy and enthusiasm, all

177

blood and silence on the forward deck, and she hurled herself forward, boat hook in hand, and thrust blindly before her into the shower of bullets.

The hook struck something and caught. There was a flat, heavy tug, like a large halibut on a line, and a kind of a gurgle. Grimly, sickly determined, Kate sawed back and forth on the pole. There was a hideous grunting sound, a clang of something metallic falling. And then silence.

Kate released a long, shuddering breath, and looked over the side of the catwalk.

The boat hook had caught Harry Gault beneath his chin, the hook penetrating up through his jaw. He stared at her, eyes wide and surprised. His mouth was slack and through his open lips she could see the bloodstained hook had penetrated the roof of his mouth.

She was afraid she was going to vomit. There was a step behind her and she felt a surge of relief. "Andy? Are you okay?"

She turned and looked straight into Seth Skinner's mild, slightly mad gray eyes.

Her mouth opened and closed. At last she said, her voice weak, "But you're in the freezer."

His mouth twisted into something that might have been a grin. "I was. Harry let me out." The grin widened. "Your turn, Katie."

He raised the monkey wrench over his head. Kate wanted to close her eyes, but she couldn't. She wanted to move, to run, but she couldn't do that either. All she could do was lie there, too exhausted to flee, too numb for fear, and watch Seth Skinner kill her.

And then Andy Pence came around the corner of the bridge with an avenging rage in his blue eyes and a feral scream ripping out of his throat and the Louisville Slugger in his hands. He brought that baseball bat down across the back of Seth Skinner's head and Seth Skinner's eyes rolled up and he went limp and he dropped the monkey wrench and he fell, heavily, across Kate's prone, unresisting body.

● ● ●

The next thing she knew Andy had her by the shoulders and was shaking her roughly. "Come on, Kate. Wake up. Wake up, dammit!"

"Andy?" she said groggily. She came upright and clutched at him. "Andy. I thought you were dead."

He grinned down at her, a fearful sight what with all the blood and swelling. "Turnabout's fair play. You okay?"

"I think so," Kate said vaguely. She couldn't look at the thing sprawled so obscenely on the deck below, the boat hook still protruding from its head. She shoved Seth's limp body farther away. "Is Seth dead?"

"Him?" Andy said contemptuously. "Not a chance. I just brained him a little. Come on, let's get you below and out of those clothes."

She shoved him away. "Take care of—take care of *it* first. Please?" she said when he would have argued with her. "Please, Andy?" She offered him a tired smile. "I'd do it myself but I don't think I can."

For all his bravado Andy stumbled a little as he produced a blanket from the chart room and tucked it around her where she sat, with her back against the bridge bulkhead. He shinnied down the ladder from the catwalk to the deck and handed her up the pistol. She held it in a loose grip, not sure she could summon up the strength to fire it if Seth woke up.

Andy produced a tarpaulin, rolled Gault's body in it and rolled the body into the fo'c'sle. Armed with Gault's pistol in one hand and the baseball bat in the other and with the biggest butcher knife in the galley clenched between his teeth, he got Ned out of the hold. Ned was numb and dazed and didn't put up much of a fight. Seth moaned when Andy dragged him by his feet down the stairs and over the raised sill of the galley door, but he, too, was safely behind the locked door of the fo'c'sle before he woke up enough to protest. Andy pushed a crab pot in front of the door to be sure, and to be surer still pushed and shoved another seven-by in front of it. Fifteen hundred pounds of insurance. He decided it was enough.

Kate watched him, sitting on the catwalk with her back against the bulkhead and her feet hanging over the edge. Andy climbed the ladder, took one hand and pulled her to her feet and hoisted her over his shoulder in a fireman's carry. In their stateroom, he stripped her down and bundled her between the covers. "I'm starting to feel like your mother," he told her.

"Can you get us back to Dutch?" she managed to ask him.

"Piece of cake,'" he said, pushing the blond thatch of hair out of his eyes. "After all, the lady's line is out, and I know my girl's been pulling on it since we left the breakwater."

"You have a girl?"

"Sure. Just haven't found her yet."

Kate smiled in spite of herself.

Before he left he pulled out his first-aid kit and rummaged through it. He held up two slender whitish rocks, flat-sided and columnar, about three inches in length. "Tabbies," he pronounced, and at her confused look elaborated, "tabular crystals." He closed her right hand around one, her left hand around the other. "A tabbie in each hand balances your energy flow and assists in communication with your higher self.

They're especially good in helping ease extreme emotional stress. Every first-aid kit should have at least two. I chose them and they know me, but they'll help you because you're my friend."

Looking up, he saw her eyes closing and broke off the lecture. "Relax," he said, patting her shoulder. "Sleep. I'll get us home."

It might have been sheer exhaustion, it might have been the tabbies. Kate slept, her last conscious sense the feel of cool quartz crystal warming to the palms of her hands.

CHAPTER 10

"SO HE BOUGHT UP a bunch of old boats with nothing down and a promise of balloon payments within six months."

"He reneged on the balloons," Kate guessed.

"Got it in one."

"When was this?"

Jack's grin widened. "April of 1989."

"Right after the RPetCo oil spill."

"I told you you'd like it."

"Gault was a spillionaire, wasn't he? He signed on with RPetCo, and his boats worked the spill."

"Got it again." Jack nodded smugly. "There's a guy at RPetCo we're talking to, seems he may have earned a little extra that summer for putting Harry's boats at the top of the hiring list. Then, when RPetCo declared the cleanup a success, Gault skipped on the mortgages, the boat crews' last paychecks, and boogied Outside. Next known address—"

"Freetown, Oregon," Kate said.

Jack cocked his thumb and fired his finger at her.

"Where he married the boss's daughter and was rewarded with a boat of his own. Nice work if you can get it." He remembered and looked as abashed as a grown man can. "Sorry, sir."

Nordensen inclined his head. "Don't be. It is the truth."

Kate thought of the freezing wind, the icy salt spray, the

slippery, shifting deck beneath her feet, tossing her cookies every two hours. Nice work if you can get it? She wouldn't go that far.

"And," Jack said lightly, recovering from his embarrassment, "as I taught you when you worked for me in the D.A.'s office, if a perp has screwed up once, it's even odds he's screwed up in a prior life."

"Don't start holding out on us now," Kate said. She was warm and full and rested for the first time in what felt like months and she didn't really care if Harry Gault had cheated on his wife, robbed his grandmother and beaten his dog all on the same day, but she summoned up a dutiful interest to keep Jack happy and the story rolling. "Tell, tell."

"There's a warrant out on one Harley Gruber in California, who matches Gault's general description."

"What's he wanted for?" Andy wanted to know.

Kate smothered a laugh and Jack grinned. "Fraud and embezzlement. Something to do with a land development deal in western San Diego."

"I thought most of western San Diego was ocean," Andy said, puzzled.

"Also, when Gruber skipped, not one, not two, but three, count 'em, three wives came forward to file claims to his estate."

"Not including the wife in Freetown, Oregon. Any kids?"

"By which wife? Guy'd been married more times than Mickey Rooney and had more kids than the King in *The King and I*."

"Poor woman," Kate said.

"Poor women," Jack said. "And this is the best part, Kate, you're going to love this. You know what Gault was doing with part of the dough he was scoring off the coke sales?"

"No," Kate said, playing along, "what was he doing, Jack?"

Jack's delighted grin almost split his face in two. "He was buying up sides of Kodiak beef, flying them down here in the Navaho and smuggling them on board Japanese processors. When they got back to Yokohama with their load of fish, whatever crew member was in on the deal would somehow smuggle the beef past customs and sell it on the black market." Jack's already wide grin widened. "You know how much beef costs per pound in a store in downtown Tokyo these days?"

"No," Kate said faintly. "How much?"

"Actually, I wasn't able to find out, either. None of the Japanese I talked to buy it at home, except in meals in restaurants. I talked to somebody at Alaska Pacific University and they told me imported beef is sold back and forth between suppliers without it ever leaving the freezer, until they can sell it for ten times what it cost them to buy it wholesale."

There was a brief, awed silence. "So if you buy a T-bone for five bucks here," Andy said, "it'll cost you fifty in Tokyo?"

"At least. You know, I've seen those Japan Air Line crews with their shopping carts full of beef at Carr's in the Sear's Mall in Anchorage. I mean full carts, too, piled right up to the top, and not just one cart, either, but three and four carts at a time. Yeah, I figure our buddy Harry was turning a tidy profit on what he made off the coke."

Kate searched for an adequate response. There wasn't one. "I told you he was greedy."

They were seated around a table at the Unisea Restaurant in Dutch Harbor, Andy and Kate hogging down the first meal in days they hadn't had to cook themselves. Jack was on Kate's right, Andy was across from her, and on her left was a man so lean and fit that at first it was not noticeable how old he was. He had a full head of hair, pure white, and small,

184

twinkling blue eyes. His name was Sten Nordensen, and he was the chairman of the board of directors for Alaska Ventures, Inc. He had flown up from Freetown, Oregon, the day before and had been waiting for the *Avilda* at the dock. Now he pushed himself a little away from the table. When he spoke his speech was slow and somewhat formal, with the faintest trace of an accent. "How can I thank you for all you have done, Miss Shugak?"

"Pay me my crew share from my last trip out," she replied promptly. "And the name's Kate."

He smiled, a grave and beautiful smile, and inclined his head. "Done, Kate. But I think we can do better than a mere crew share."

"Okay," she said, agreeable. She pointed her fork across the table. "After you refit the *Avilda*, hire Andy on the crew."

Andy flushed up to the roots of his hair and looked nine instead of nineteen.

"He got us back in one piece," she told Nordensen. "I was incapable."

"You would have been capable if you'd had to be," Andy mumbled.

"He got us back," Kate said, ignoring Andy and concentrating on the old man. "With less experience at the helm and in navigation than a newborn baby he got us back five hundred miles to Dutch, got us inside the harbor and got us safely moored. I was out cold the whole time. He may lack experience but he's a natural born boat jockey, Mr. Nordensen. Don't let him get away."

Nordensen looked at Andy reflectively. "For one who has done my company such a great service, a place can be found."

Andy flushed again. His mouth opened and closed a few times before he managed to say, "Thank you, sir." The look he sent across the table contained such burning gratitude that Kate felt singed.

"Ned Nordhoff's rolling over like a dog in dirt," Jack said, reapplying himself to his steak with vigor. "Too bad Harry's dead, we coulda locked him up until the United States elects a woman president." He looked over at Kate, wondering if the mention of Harry Gault's death would upset her.

Kate, puzzled, said, "Why's he talking? Harry's dead. All Ned has to do is say it was all Harry's fault and claim he was a victim of circumstance."

Nope, Jack decided. The *Avilda*'s late skipper had been trying to kill her. She had been protecting herself, as well as this weird blond kid whom she seemed to have adopted. She wasn't likely to be suffering any repressed guilt over Harry Gault's grisly end. Hers would have been grislier. Squashing that thought with more haste than finesse, he produced a smile no one noticed was a little frayed around the edges. "I do believe someone may have hinted that Seth Skinner was doing some talking of his own."

"And is he?"

Jack cut another piece from his steak with absorbed precision. "Now there is a strange one. I can't figure him out. He won't say a word, not even when I told him Ned was singing on key nonstop with no time out for intermissions or encores. He won't talk to us, he won't talk to an attorney. He just sits there."

"He can sit there and rot until he croaks," Kate said cordially. "And I for one hope he does."

Andy shook his head reprovingly. "The One Way teaches us to strive for right thinking and right action in this life, to earn a better life in the next. Harry and Ned and Seth will pay for their wrong thinking and their wrong action in the next

186

life. It is written, 'Just as a man casts off worn-out clothes and takes on others that are new, so the embodied soul casts off worn-out bodies and takes on others that are new. The soul in the body of everyone is eternal and indestructible. Therefore thou shouldst not mourn for any creature.'"

"And in particular not for this one," Jack said under his breath.

"Then let's hope they all come back as tanner crab," Kate said, "and have to work their way up from there." She hoped Andy hadn't queered Nordensen's job offer. She turned and said brightly, "I hear you've got a new ship coming off the ways any day now, Mr. Nordensen."

The old man gave a proud nod. "That we do."

"What's the latest one's name?" Kate said. "The *Mary Lovell,* wasn't it? The *Avilda,* the *Madame Ching,* the *Anne Bonney.* And now the *Mary Lovell.* Beautiful names. You have plans for a *Grace O'Malley* in the future?"

He inclined his head again. "She is already designed."

Their eyes met and Kate, seeing the twinkle in the blue gaze, was unable to repress a laugh.

Jack and Andy exchanged mystified glances. "What's so funny?"

"Shall you tell them, or shall I?" Kate asked Nordensen.

The old man smiled and shook his head.

Kate turned back to Jack. "They were all pirates."

Jack and Andy looked confused, and she said, chuckling, "Avilda. Grace O'Malley. Mary Read and Lady Killigrew and Anne Bonney and Madame Ching and Mary Lovell. Pirates, all of them."

"You're kidding." Jack looked at the old man but Nordensen just grinned at him.

"Nope," Kate said, wiping her mouth and sitting back in

her chair. "I went over to the library at the Unalaska School this morning and looked them up in the encyclopedia. Avilda was some kind of Viking, Grace and Lady Killigrew terrorized the English Channel, Mary and Anne shot up the Caribbean with Morgan and Blackbeard, and Madame Ching thought the South China Sea was her own private lake. Alaska Ventures's boats are all named after lady pirates."

"Some of them not so much the lady," Nordensen reminded her.

"No kidding," she said, "Grace O'Malley's son fell overboard once and she was so angry at his clumsiness that she chopped off his hands with a knife when he tried to climb back on board."

Jack threw back his head and roared, and after a stunned moment Andy joined in.

When the laughter died down Kate said, "What's our new best friend Ned say about the dope dealing? How'd that get started?"

"From what our new best friend Ned says, Gault's connections had been landing wholesale quantities of cocaine on Anua ever since Gault began working these waters. His crew members had been going ashore to pick them up." Jack looked across the table at Nordensen. "I'm sorry, sir, I know this is the last thing you want to hear, but according to Nordhoff, Alcala and Brown were up to their ears in the dope dealing. They got greedy, started siphoning off grams and grams and stashing them around the airstrip. Their plan was to fly in with their own plane, once they got back to port, and pick it up. Gault was suspicious and followed them in—cutting that barge loose, by the way, that's when he lost it—and caught them at it and killed them in the act."

"Who died in the dugout?" Kate asked.

"*Barabara*" Jack said.

"Whatever."

He smiled. "Alcala. He ran when Gault and Nordhoff caught him and Brown at the airstrip."

"Who killed him?"

"Skinner."

Kate was unsurprised. It would take a long time for her to forget the sound of Seth's voice coaxing her out of the canned goods, the indifferent mad look in his serene eyes as he raised the monkey wrench over his head. "And the slug we found?"

"From a .38 Skinner tossed over the side."

"And the bodies?"

"Wired inside a crab pot and over the side."

Nordensen spoke without looking up. "Any kind of a bearing where they went over?"

Jack shook his head. "I'm afraid not, sir. They could be anywhere between here and Anua. There's no way of knowing. And what with Aleutian weather..."

To his plate, Nordensen said softly, "It will be difficult for their families. First the drugs, then no possible hope of recovery of the bodies." He looked up, his face grave. "Yes, it will be very difficult."

Kate thought of the two young faces that had haunted her days on the *Avilda*. Victims or dealers? This time, both. She couldn't find it in her to condemn them too harshly. Wrong boat, wrong crew, wrong time. The money had come to them so quickly, more money than they'd ever seen for a day's work, a week's, a month's.

A season later and they were forty thousand to the good, but it wasn't easy money. Kate thought of the night of ice again and shivered. No, not easy. At least when you were dealing you were dry and warm and didn't miss any meals. It must have looked like a cakewalk by comparison.

"So," Jack was saying, "Harry cooked up that story about going ashore for water and getting lost in the storm to cover what really happened."

The waiter came by with a coffeepot and they waited until he refilled their cups. "And why not? Who was there to say otherwise? Ned and Seth were in his pocket, the guys on the plane were in partnership with him, God knows the Aleutians have taken more than their share of human life. He didn't even have to fear the *Avilda* being taken away from him, what with his advantageous—and convenient—marriage." Jack inclined his head. "Sorry again, sir."

"Why?" Nordensen said, this time with a touch of weary resignation. "I should never have let my daughter marry him. I knew it was wrong, I knew *he* was wrong." He shrugged. "But she had been a widow for so long, and she said she loved him, and I loved her too much to say no."

Silence grew around the table, until Jack, appalled, said slowly, "You didn't tell me it was your daughter he married, Mr. Nordensen."

The old man smiled a bleak, wintry smile. "And advertise my own stupidity?" He rose to his feet, Andy and Jack rising with him. He reached for Kate's hand and with Old World charm bowed over it, brushing the back of it lightly with his lips. "Again, Kate, my thanks. With great initiative, and at tremendous personal risk you have found out the truth, brought the criminals to account for their actions and restored the *Avilda* to our fleet. Alaska Ventures will never be able to repay what it owes you." His eyes twinkled. "But we will try. Your check will be ready to be picked up tomorrow."

Kate, caught by surprise with her mouth full of baked potato, gulped and said indistinctly, "Thank you, sir."

He released her hand and said to Andy, "I'm spending the next week here in Dutch Harbor until my crew flies up from Freetown. I'll be bunking in the captain's cabin. You will keep your own berth, please. I will expect to see you at breakfast tomorrow, when we will talk."

Andy stammered out his thanks and they all watched the tall, erect old man walk out of the restaurant.

Kate looked down at her clean plate and heaved a sigh for all good things past. Catching sight of the clock on the wall, she pushed back her chair and rose to her feet. "It's time, guys."

They followed her out of the restaurant and into the truck Jack had commandeered from some poor cannery schmuck who didn't know any better. They drove to Unalaska and parked near the white frame building, perched within sight and sound of the lap of the waves and crowned with onion domes. A crowd was gathering before the church, and they climbed out and joined it. Kate saw villagers and fishermen and cannery workers, skippers and deckhands, processors and packers, standing shoulder to shoulder in clusters around the little church. Japanese stood next to Koreans, Koreans next to Chinese, Chinese next to Americans, Americans next to Aleuts. They were all men and women of the sea, all there for the same reason, to propitiate whatever the gods might be for a good catch and a safe journey home.

The Russians were there, too, unsurprising since Kate had seen the *Ekaterina* in the harbor that morning.

"Kate!" Anatoly shouldered his way through the crowd and swept her up into an exuberant embrace, kissing her smackingly on both cheeks and taking a longer and less smacking time over her mouth. Next to them Jack stood up a little straighter.

Anatoly let her go and said anxiously, "Kate? All right are you, yes? Things hear I in Dutch, not good for you."

"I'm fine, but, Anatoly, you're speaking English!"

He beamed and produced a decrepit, leather-bound Russian-English dictionary with half the pages falling out that must have been published when the *promishlyniki* first came to Alaska. "Study I, yes? Speak I good?"

This last was said with such anxiety that Kate didn't have the heart to disillusion him. "Of course you do. You speak very well."

He beamed again and might have swept her up into another exuberant embrace if Jack hadn't cleared his throat in a manner that needed no translation. With reluctance Anatoly let Kate go.

An old, old man in a long, elaborately embroidered robe appeared on the steps of the church. He had a grizzled beard that reached almost to his knees, enormous, bushy eyebrows that cast deep shadows over his eyes, and a dignified, authoritative presence that immediately stilled the whispers and rustling of the congregation.

"I had no idea so many Aleuts were Russian Orthodox," Jack whispered.

"It was the only sensible thing to do," Kate whispered back. "When the first priests came to Alaska, every Aleut who agreed to be baptized in the Russian Orthodox faith was exempted from three years' worth of taxes."

Jack turned his laugh into a cough as the patriarch began to speak. They celebrated mass there, out in the open, partly because there wasn't room for them all in the church, but Kate thought mostly so that they could be closer to the sea, so He would make no mistake about what they were asking His blessing for.

The Russian Orthodox patriarch was very specific. He asked God to make the fishermen wise and strong. He asked that their boats be sound and seaworthy. He asked that the sea be fruitful. He reminded Him that the *opilio* and king crab seasons were about to open, and asked His blessing on the catch. He mentioned the weather only in passing, as if aware that even the power of God went only so far.

The bell in the steeple began to ring. One for each fisherman dead in the past season. Kate counted forty-one. Forty-one fishermen lost to the Cradle of the Winds since last year's Blessing of the Sea. It would have been forty, but for Harry Gault. She searched herself for guilt, and found none. He would have killed her without compunction, and Andy, too. The memory of the inside of that steel cage, of the rapid descent into a cold, green grave, was all too vivid. Deliberately she shook it off. Harry was dead but she was alive. Andy was alive. She raised her head to draw cool fog and salt air deep into her lungs, and expelled it on a long, slow, almost voluptuous sigh. Jack squeezed her hand and she smiled without looking at him.

The last peal died away and they stood in silence. The fog drifted offshore, muting the coming and going of boats, the noise of the processing plants across Iliuliuk Bay, the inevitable stutter of the taxi vans passing back and forth. Andy, rapt and reverent throughout the service, gave a long, deep sigh. "Did you ever hear of Deva Lokka?" he asked her in a low, dreamy voice.

She shook her head.

"She's the Hindu goddess of death. She waits at the bottom of the sea for sailors who drown."

Kate looked blank. "Deva Lokka," he prompted. "Get it? Deva Lokka. Davy Jones's locker."

The patriarch raised his hand in the sign of the cross, in the name of the Father and the Son and the Holy Ghost. As the mass ended Kate felt a touch on her arm and turned to see Olga, a scarf tied over her head and Sasha at her side. "Hello, Auntie."

"Hello, Kate," Olga replied. They moved out of the crowd, and stood side by side looking out at the water. "Didn't I tell you? When the killer whales come."

"When the killer whales come," Kate agreed, and surprised both of them by reaching out and enveloping the other woman in a fierce hug.

She would have hugged Sasha, too, but the girl pulled out the storyknife and walked down to the beach to squat in the sand. Kate followed and squatted next to her. "Another story, Sasha? What is it this time?"

Sasha drew a symbol and touched it delicately with the point of the knife. "Woman," she said sternly, looking at Kate.

"Woman," Kate said, nodding.

Sasha drew the figure with eight arms. "Bad."

"Monster," Kate said, nodding again.

"Bad," Sasha said firmly.

Kate gave an involuntary laugh. "Okay, you're telling this story. Bad."

Sasha enclosed both figures in two concentric circles. "Home." In the quick, deft, graceful gestures that were such a painful contrast to the rest of her clumsy, shambling movements, Sasha sketched in a river and drew lines first from the woman to the river, and then the bad to the river.

"The bad is chasing the woman? To the river?"

Sasha nodded, still drawing.

Kate watched the little figures appear and disappear and reappear in the sand. "The bad chasing the woman. The woman crossing the river. The bad crossing the river, too."

Sasha nodded her head fiercely. She pointed to the woman and to the river, with the bad still in the river.

"The woman looks at the river? She looks at the bad?" Sasha looked annoyed and Kate was ashamed of her obtuseness.

Sasha tilted her head back and held her cupped hand up to her mouth, pantomiming drinking. "Glug, glug, glug."

Light broke. "She drinks the river."

Sasha shook her head. "She doesn't drink the river." Sasha pantomimed drinking again and pointed from herself pantomiming to the woman. "Oh, she pretends to drink the river, like you're pretending. Why?"

Sasha pointed to the bad. "She tells the bad she drinks the river?" Sasha pointed from one side of the river to the other. "She tells the bad she drank the river and that was how she got across!"

A wide smile broke across Sasha's face, lighting the heavy, unformed features with humor and intelligence. She pointed to the bad and pantomimed drinking.

"So the bad tries to drink the water so he can get across."

With one stroke of the knife Sasha made the sign for death below the bad. Above it, she made the sign for thunderbird.

"So the bad dies from drinking too much river, and the thunderbird comes and takes his body away to feed to its children."

Sasha showed the thunderbird flying off to its volcanic nest, the bad clutched in its claws, and the woman figure on her merry way. Smoothing the sand clear with a flourish, she sat back on her heels and looked expectantly at Kate.

Kate smiled at her. "It's a wonderful story, Sasha. Thank you for telling it to me."

Sasha's eyebrows met in a straight line. "No. No no no."

"What?" Kate said. "What's the matter? Didn't I get it right?"

Sasha pointed from the woman figure to Kate. "Woman. You. Woman. Woman dead bad. You. Woman. Dead. Bad." Her hand came out and gripped Kate's shoulder. "You. Woman. Good."

Kate could find nothing to say.

Sasha gave a satisfied nod. Sheathing her storyknife, she struggled to her feet, and vanished down the beach and into the mist.

"Kate?" Jack's voice said from somewhere behind her. "You coming?"

She found her eyes had filled with tears. Impatiently she blinked them back and stood up. "Yes. I'm coming."

AFTERWORD

April 2011

Until I proofed this manuscript for the Gere Donovan e-publication, I'd forgotten how much of my own life experiences I had incorporated into it. I spent five years of my childhood on a 75-foot fish tender named the *Celtic*, in Cook Inlet and Prince William Sound, and a lot of the detail in this book is verbatim from that time—as much crab as you wanted anytime you wanted it fresh out of the water, the walk-in freezers, the fo'c'sle full of canned goods, the build-up of homicidal ice on the deck.

That first chapter? Yes, I have been that seasick. One time we were coming around Port Dick in an October storm and the boat was heeling so far over on its sides that the view through the porthole over my bunk switched from all water to all sky to all water to all sky, over and over again, for what seemed like forever.

A couple of hours later my mom came down from the wheelhouse and I was no longer in my bunk. She was panic-stricken, she was terrified I'd gone out on deck and fallen overboard. She ransacked the staterooms, the head, even the engine room, and then she found me curled up on the deck beneath the galley table, where I'd wrapped myself around the center leg.

Make a fist and rock it back and forth. The center of your fist is going to be the place of least motion. The center leg of the table, which was in the center of the galley, which was on the main deck, was the place of least motion during the storm that poor little nine-year-old girl could find. Mom brought me a pillow and a blanket and left me there until we made Picnic Harbor. To this day Picnic Harbor is still my favorite fjord anywhere on the Alaskan coast.

If you've ever seen "The Deadliest Catch" on the Discovery Channel and thought some or all of that was special effects: It isn't. There's a reason those guys make that much money. There is also a reason why no one writes actuarial tables on Bering Sea crab fishermen. Insurance companies won't insure them. It's way too easy to die doing what they do.

One of my proudest moments as an author was when a Kodiak crab fisherman called my dad in Anchorage (he was in the phone book and he fielded a lot of calls concerning me). The fisherman had just read and he wanted to tell me how much he'd liked the book, and compliment me on how much I'd gotten right.

Another reason I'm a writer is because I never wanted to do his job.

MAP OF NINILTNA

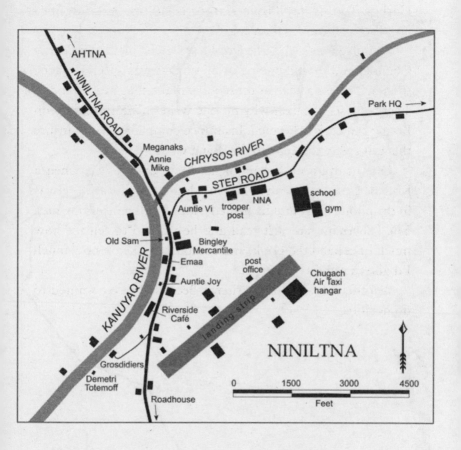

MAP OF THE PARK

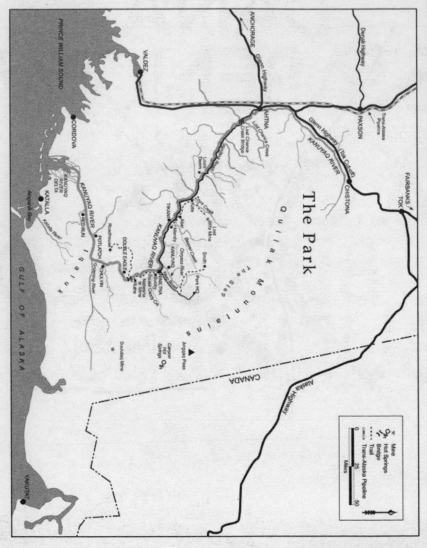

MAPS BY DR CHERIE NORTHON

WWW.MAPMAKERS.COM

A KATE SHUGAK INVESTIGATION

4

DANA STABENOW

'UNIQUE IN THE CROWDED FIELD OF CRIME FICTION' MICHAEL CONNELLY

A COLD BLOODED BUSINESS

Someone is selling drugs to the employees of a Prudhoe Bay oil field company. Kate Shugak is tasked to go undercover and apprehend the dealer...

INTRODUCTION

Did I see a pipeliner pull a grizzly bear's tail in Prudhoe Bay?
   No.
   I saw a pipeliner pull a grizzly bear's tail at Galbraith Lake
Pipeline Camp.
   Seriously. I couldn't make that up, my imagination isn't
that good. Nearly all the events described herein really did
happen, including the turtle races. I was there. I saw them.
   I spend four months in 1975 working on the TransAlaska
Pipeline for Alyeska at Galbraith, and the following year went
to work for BP at Prudhoe Bay. I went because it was where
all the best stories were coming from, not to mention the best
paychecks. Alaskans of my generation had never seen money
like that in our lives and we were all filling out applications at
Arco and BP and Veco and paying Dobie dues down at the
Teamster's Union. Yes, I saw guys playing check poker with
twelve-hundred dollar checks. What the hell, there'd be
another one just like it next week.
   I only meant to stay a year, but BP kept promoting me to
better jobs at higher pay, so I stayed for six. I had Toni
Hartzler's job in the end, tour guide for the Western Operating
Area, aka the BP side. I picked up state supreme court justices
and Exxon boards of directors and engineers and architects
and shareholders and spouses and ferried them around the
Slope by the van- and busload. Most of the ignorant questions

I was asked are immortalized in *A Cold-Blooded Business*. Like I said, I couldn't make this stuff up.

A few years back an Anchorage bookseller told me a story about a guy coming into her store, looking for more of my books. He was a Sloper and he'd just read *A Cold-Blooded Business*. "She even knows where the lights switches are!" he said.

Bet your ass I do.

AUTHOR'S NOTE

This book is a work of fiction. There's no such man as John King. There is no RPetCo. There were never any drugs at Prudhoe Bay. There wasn't any booze, either. Nobody ever wrapped duct tape around the TransAlaska Pipeline; turtles never raced at the Base Camp; two women never sold $20,000 worth of magazine subscriptions in two days at Crazyhorse; nobody's ever sold Native American artifacts to the Detroit Institute of Arts for $55,000; no oil company ever spilled ten million gallons of oil into Prince William Sound; and I've got some land for sale in Wasilla, guaranteed swamp-free, beneath which Arco's about to find a natural gas field the size of the Sadlerochit.

CHAPTER 1

"HI, JOHN. Here she is."

The man on the couch met Mutt's yellow eyes and his ruddy face lost color. "Jesus H. Christ on a crutch."

Jack grinned. He was a big man and it was a big grin. "Not her." He jerked his thumb over his shoulder. "Her."

Her five-foot self barely visible behind Jack's six-foot-two mass, Kate closed the door and dumped her duffel on the floor.

The man on the couch wasn't looking at anything but Mutt. "What the hell is this, that's a goddam wolf, Morgan!"

Jack gave his stock answer. "Nah. Only half. Mutt, John King." Kate stepped around Jack. "Kate Shugak, John King. John's the CEO of the Alaskan division of RPetCo, the operator for the western half of the Prudhoe Bay field." A second man standing next to the couch received a perfunctory wave of the hand. "Lou Childress, RPetCo's security chief. You know who Kate is, gentlemen."

King glowered from Kate to Mutt and back again. He wasn't accustomed to being thrown off balance and he didn't like it. "About goddam time," he said curtly. Mutt lifted a lip at his tone, but King ignored her, if anyone on two legs can truly ignore the weighty gaze of a 140-pound half husky, half wolf, and concentrated on the woman.

She gave an impression of height, possibly because she held

her spine so straight, possibly because her gaze was so level and direct. Her shoulders were squared, her waist narrow and her hair reached it in a straight, black fall. Her face was broad with high cheekbones, her mouth full-lipped and wide. Held straight and unsmiling, it made her look aloof, even severe. A hint of epicanthic fold between brow and lash slanted over clear hazel eyes that went oddly with the rest of her coloring. Their expression was cool and measuring, containing a speculation devoid of curiosity. Her skin was a rich, golden brown, smooth and unlined, and the only warm thing about her. It looked younger than the thirty-two years Jim Chopin had told him she was.

Her eyes looked older. A lot older.

Jack repeated, "Kate Shugak, John King."

She was shrugging out of her jacket. King let his eyes wander down to the open collar of her shirt and he saw the scar, a knotted cord of paler flesh pulling at that otherwise smooth, perfect skin. He knew the story, of course. Chopper Jim's briefing had been concise but thorough, the direct result of RPetCo buying every Alaska state trooper's raffle ticket that came their way, and encouraging a similar habit in RPetCo's 1,500 statewide employees and 3,000 contractors.

She stood, hands at her sides, waiting impassively. "How do," he said shortly, and held out a hand.

They shook without speaking as she looked him over with the same frankness he had her. He was six inches taller than she was and had the same general build as a fireplug with a square face and fair, freckled skin that flushed easily. He had no discernible neck and thick, straight blond hair that fell in his eyes and over his collar. His glasses were wire-rimmed and thick-lensed and magnified the baleful glare that appeared to be his natural expression. The result would have a daunting effect on anyone across a negotiating table or on the carpet in front of him. She wondered if that was why he wore them. His frayed, faded jeans were rolled up twice at the cuffs over mustard-yellow cowboy boots, and his plaid shirt strained to contain his barrel-shaped chest.

Kate sat opposite him and Jack went into the kitchen. He opened the refrigerator and gazed inside as if it might hold the ultimate answer to the mystery of the universe. "Want a refill on that beer, John? Kate? You thirsty?"

"You got any Diet 7UP?"

"Nope. Pepsi, root beer, Coors, that's it."

"A glass of ice water then."

John King gave a snort clearly audible to Jack two rooms away. "I'll have another beer myself."

"So will I," Childress said immediately, and sat down next to John King. He was easier to pigeonhole than King, but the ability to do it gave Kate no pleasure. Brush cut, knife-sharp creases in his tailored slacks, black loafers shined so brightly she could see her reflection in them from ten paces. His tie was squared away in the best military fashion, his shirt a breastplate of starch, his expression D.I.-certified hostile. Retired military, had to be, and probably, God help her, Marine. She looked for flaws in the government-issue facade and found only one. Seated, an incipient potbelly that she was ready to bet Childress fought every meal of his life spilled over a tightly clinched, gleaming leather belt. For the rest, he was a paragon of God and country; tight-lipped and a tighter ass. Already she was bored.

He looked her over, too, but he was so annoyed that she'd beaten him to it that his perusal was less effective. She waited, dispassionate, until he looked up to meet her eyes. "Childress."

His nod was curt. "Shugak." He slapped shut a manila file

folder and tossed it into the eelskin briefcase open on the coffee table. "John, I want to go on record one more time as being against this. My department can resolve this thing internally."

"Your objection is noted," John King growled.

Kate propped her feet on the coffee table and said nothing.

The silence in the living room reached into the kitchen, where Jack dropped ice cubes into a glass, filled it and a large bowl with water, grabbed the beer bottles by their necks and juggled everything into the living room. Kate was seated on the loveseat across from John King, both of them working at not being the first to blink, while Childress practiced scowling and from one side Mutt observed the staring match with all the bored disinterest of a professional witnessing an amateur event. Jack bit back a smile and set the bowl down next to her and handed the glass of water to Kate. John King drank half his beer in one long swallow as Jack eased gratefully into an easy chair and put the footrest up. The chair gave a protesting groan but held.

John King burped, and gave the bottle a look of disgust. "Might's well be drinking sody pop." He drained it with another gulp and set the empty bottle down with a snap. Childress set his, barely tasted, next to King's. King transferred his look of disgust to Kate. "What's your fee?"

It was more of an attack than an inquiry. Keeping her tone mild, Kate replied, "Seven hundred fifty a day, plus expenses."

King snorted. Childress did, too, but it was an action unsuited to his high, thin, aristocratic nose. For King it was more natural, an all-purpose expression denoting disbelief, contempt and ridicule at will, singly or all together. "You get four hundred a day, when you're working, which Chopper Jim says ain't all that often."

Her expression didn't change. "For Royal Petroleum Company, majority partner in the Prudhoe Bay oil field and producer of fourteen percent of the nation's oil supply, my price is seven-fifty a day. Plus expenses."

He snorted again. So did Childress, who said, "You won't have any expenses. We provide food, lodging and arctic gear, and you ride to work on our own charter. All you have to do is investigate."

The last word was something between a sneer and a snarl, and Kate examined him thoughtfully. Jack watched Lou Childress try not to squirm beneath that cool survey, and had to give him an A for effort.

Kate let the silence get uncomfortable before breaking it. "What's the job?"

Again, King's question was more of a bark than a question. "What do you know about Prudhoe Bay?"

She linked her hands behind her head and leaned back. "It's a super-giant oil formation producing a million and a half barrels of oil per day, the largest oil field in North America. It sits on the edge of the Arctic Ocean 600 miles north of Anchorage, 250 miles north of the Arctic Circle, 100 miles north of the Brooks Range and 1,300 miles south of the geographic North Pole. It runs about 125,000 square acres in size, with, lately, around 4,000-plus employees. There are two operating owners, Royal Petroleum Company, aka RPetCo, and American Exploration, aka Amerex. You've been taking the oil out since, oh, since when, since 1976 or thereabouts. The field should have begun to decline in 1986 but due to new recovery techniques and the exploitation of several smaller fields in the vicinity, this decline has been delayed."

"First oil into OCC in Valdez was July 28, 1977," King corrected her, but he couldn't hide his surprise.

8

One corner of her mouth drew up. "I'm an Alaska Native, King. I was born and raised and I live in the Bush. We've got a new school in my village, with a brand-new gymnasium tacked on, and a brand-new power plant to keep the lights on during the Class C state championships. I'm well aware they were paid for with state taxes on Prudhoe Bay crude." She also had clear and distinct memories of what it was like trying to dribble a basketball outside at twenty below, but she saw no reason to say so.

"Taxes increased eleven times in twelve years by the Alaska state legislature," he said immediately.

Kate declined to debate the average I.Q. in Juneau. "What's the job?"

He pushed his jaw out. "One thing I gotta know up front before this goes any further. How do you feel about the oil business in Alaska?"

She knew instantly what he was getting at. "Don't you mean, how do I feel about the oil business in Alaska after the *RPetCo Anchorage* spill?" The answer was obvious on his face, and she said, "I think I'm more interested in why RPetCo hired a known drunk to steer a day's production of Prudhoe crude through the Valdez Narrows in a Very Large Crude Carrier, when two states had already yanked his license to drive a car. And I'm definitely interested in the fact that he's still working for RPetCo." Her smile was slight and humorless. "Training new tanker crews."

Childress stirred but King beat him to it. "He ain't working for RPetCo, he's working for the seamen's union. We don't got nothing to do with that."

Out of the loop, Jack thought, and wondered if John King knew George Bush from his wildcatting days in Texas. He took a sip of beer, savoring it all the way down.

"And he *was* acquitted," John King added. Kate said nothing, and he was driven to fill the sudden vacuum. "Well? I know your homestead's close to the Gulf of Alaska. You gotta have friends, relatives, who were affected by the spill." Still Kate didn't answer, and goaded, John King declared, "I gotta tell you, I'm of half a mind to do like Lou says, let his department take care of this. I don't like the idea of sending a broad in on a job like this, let alone a Native broad. But Morgan says you're the best investigator he ever had in the D.A.'s office. Chopper Jim backs him up. Shit, even the fucking FBI says you're good."

"An unimpeachable source of information," Kate murmured. "Look at all they've done for Leonard Peltier."

"Okay." King's voice rose. "I just don't want you busting my chops after the fact with whatever dirt you dish up on my people down the line, just because you think you've got an axe to grind because you're a Native or a woman or because you think all the oil companies ought to have their asses kicked back Outside where they belong. I want this kept quiet. I got enough problems already without broadcasting the fact that half my people are putting their paychecks up their noses." He realized what he'd said too late and his mouth snapped shut with an audible click.

Jack studied his beer bottle thoughtfully. John King had all the social skills of a blast furnace.

Kate took a long swallow of water and set the glass down carefully on the coffee table. "My fee is seven-fifty a day." She looked at Childress. "Plus expenses." She looked back at King. "Your checks don't bounce, that buys you a fair amount of discretion." For the third and last time, she said, "What's the job?"

As he met that unblinking hazel stare, John King

10

remembered something Gamble, the federal agent, had said. *She's about as friendly as a double-bladed axe, but if she says she'll do a job, the job gets done. It'll cost you,* he'd added, *but it'll get done.*

At that moment John King would have sold his soul for a done job. He made up his mind. "Somebody's dealing drugs on my dime," he said bluntly. Childress gave an involuntary sound of distress. "Shut up, Lou. There've been half a dozen overdoses in the last three months." When her expression didn't change, he added, "And one death."

Kate's eyes widened. "You didn't tell me there had been a death," she told Jack.

He held his bottle to the light and inspected it for flaws. "Didn't know when I talked to you Friday at Bobby's that there'd been one."

"When did it happen?"

John King looked at Childress. "Saturday night," Childress said reluctantly, still scowling. "His body was found Sunday morning, floating facedown in the pool."

That got Kate's attention, but not in quite the way John King would have liked. "'In the *pool*'?" She looked at John King with an incredulity that wasn't entirely feigned. "You've got a swimming pool on the North Slope?"

"It doubles as a fire water reservoir," he growled.

"Of course it does," she agreed with a cordiality that set his teeth on edge. "Cocaine?" He nodded curtly. "What, was it pure and he couldn't handle it? Or is somebody cutting it with Borax?"

He shrugged impatient shoulders. "I don't know and I don't care."

"Any indications the death was not accidental?"

Childress went into orbit. "Jesus Christ, John! I've had

11

about enough of this crap! She's never even been on the Slope and now she's got crazed murderers running around the Base Camp bumping people off! I told you this could get out of hand! I—"

"Show her what you got, Lou."

"John!"

"Show her, goddammit!"

The security man's jaw clenched and his lips tightened into a thin line. After a long, tense moment he produced a small manila envelope and emptied it out on the coffee table.

Kate leaned forward to pick one of the items up. It was a creased square of waxed paper, folded into a tiny homemade envelope. She raised an eyebrow at Jack and he nodded. "That's how they're packaging the hits."

"The stewards swept up those last weekend in the common rooms of the Base Camp," John King told her, "and Christ knows that can't be even a fraction of the total." A sudden weariness assailed him, and he rubbed his hands over his face. "It hasn't been this bad since construction." He dropped his hands and glared at her accusingly. "I want it stopped."

"What's the problem? Jack was telling me on the way here that Anchorage International was rated in the top ten for best airport security in the nation last year. Sic them on it."

"We have," John King said grimly. "It's still getting through."

"Then go at it from the other end, set up a checkpoint at Prudhoe. It's your oil field, you ought to be able to exert some kind of control over what comes in."

King snorted and Childress took over. "Deadhorse," the security chief said with awful sarcasm, "is a public airport. It has three commercial carriers flying in, besides the RPetCo and Amerex charters. Not to mention the jets of every

12

corporation flush enough to float a rubbernecker for their board. Not to mention government amphibs bringing up U.S. senators and congressmen to go fishing in the Arctic National Wildlife Refuge. Not to mention one hundred fifty trucks up the haul road every month. Not to mention the six Native villages within snowmobile or outboard or Super Cub range."

He stopped, looking at John King, who was glowering at Kate, who was smart enough not to take it personally. "Drugs are coming into the Base Camp and the Western Operating Area, Shugak. *My* Base Camp and *my* Western Operating Area. Somebody's importing that shit wholesale and retailing it to *my* people and I want it stopped. I want it stopped fast, and I want it stopped now, before some asshole who should know better gets higher than a kite and bumps into the wrong valve in Skid 14 and sends a fucking production center into fucking orbit and shuts the whole fucking line down!" He was shouting before he came to the end of his sentence, his face mottled purple with rage.

She reached for her water, sipped and rolled the glass back and forth between her palms. "All right."

Breathing heavily, he stared at her. "All right?" he said, unconsciously mimicking her calm tone.

She raised her eyes from her glass and met his. "All right, I'll do it."

It was nearly impossible to get John King off the attack once he'd begun a charge. "You sure you can handle it?" he shot at her.

"Yes."

"You'll be working a week on, a week off." He gave Jack an unfriendly look. "I wanted you up straight through until you caught the fuckers, but Morgan says that'd jeopardize your cover. You'll be hired on through UCo, can you—"

"UCo?" Kate said sharply. "Who's them? I thought I was going up for RPetCo."

John King shook his head. "All our roustabouts are contract hires nowadays. Saves on paying benefits. Universal Oilfield Service Company's our main contractor, and if I'm right and I usually am"—his glare dared her to contradict him—"if I'm right, the drugs are coming in in some contract hire's toolbox and going out into the field the same way." His fists clenched and his face reddened. "I want you to go through UCo like crap through a goose. It's gotta be them. Those fucking contractors are about as loyal to the brand as Billy the Kid."

Kate wondered how much of that was the truth and how much wishful thinking, but she held her peace.

"You'll be hired on as a roustabout, which ain't a goddam Elvis movie. A roustabout does every dirty job that comes along, from signing out tools to running parts to driving bus to wellhead cleanup to picking up garbage. You seem in good shape." He looked her over critically, and this time it was a look devoid of that congenital speculation of when and how he'd get her into the sack intrinsic in any first meeting between any human male and any female who rejoiced in a functioning pulse. "But I'm here to tell you, lady, that you'd better *be* fit if you're gonna be outside at forty below in a fifteen-knot wind, humping a drill bit off the back of a pickup truck. Can you drive a pickup truck?" Jack rolled his eyes. Kate nodded. "A flatbed?" She nodded. "A bus?" She nodded again, lying this time. At this point if he'd asked her if she could launch a Saturn V rocket her answer would have been the same.

"Roustabouts' regular rotation day is Tuesday, which means you fly to Prudhoe Tuesday morning and back to Anchorage the following Tuesday afternoon. That means you leave here day after tomorrow. Got a problem with that?"

"No."

"It's one woman to five men in the Base Camp. The rest of the time you'll be out in the field where the ratio's more like ten to one and some of the guys working construction been up there since Christmas and you're gonna look like a stocking stuffer to them. Think you can handle that?"

As he spoke, John King looked at Jack Morgan, a shaggy, dark-haired, amiable giant who was the chief investigator for the Anchorage D.A. He didn't look like he could muster up enough energy to get out of his own way, but his reputation as an investigator was rock solid, even if he did look more like Paul Bunyan than Sam Spade. King looked from Morgan to Shugak and remembered something else Gamble had said. *There's something going on there. I don't know what it is, and I don't think they do, either, but don't get between them. It could be hazardous to your health.* King set his jaw. He wasn't going to take back a by-God word.

It wasn't necessary. Morgan looked even more imperturbable than Shugak, possibly even more so than that damn dog. Maybe it was a family trait. "Well?" he demanded. "You think you can handle it?"

Kate wondered if she should tell King about her last job, on a crabber in the middle of the Bering Sea, all her crewmates male, including her bunkie, three of them with murder, not seduction, on their minds. She nodded instead. It was easier.

"You better be sure, Shugak. You better be awful goddam sure. I want that fucking dope off my Slope." He subjected her to another long glare, which she endured without flinching. He transferred the glare to Jack. "You sure you can't send up one of your own?"

Without heat, Jack said, "What I said before still goes. We

15

don't have the personnel available to work the caseload in town and mount a full-scale investigation on the Slope at the same time. When Kate turns up some solid evidence, then we can move in officially. But not before."

Kate could almost hear the wheels in John King's head turn to the last ratchet, engage and lock. "All right. I still don't like it, Shugak, but you're the best I can come up with. Lou's got the address. Be there at eight tomorrow morning for orientation." Childress passed a slip of paper across the coffee table, holding it by the tips of his fingers, looking as if he wanted to hold his nose. "One more thing," King said. "Can you pass a drug screen?"

For the first time Kate lost some of her composure. "I beg your pardon?"

Her voice was a rasping growl of sound and King's eyes dropped once again to the white, twisted scar that ran across her throat literally from ear to ear. The tense set of his shoulders eased for the first time in months. Someone who had survived an attack that vicious, and had disposed so speedily and efficiently of her attacker, wasn't likely to keel over the first time a horny Sloper made a heavy-handed pass. She might just do, at that. "You'll have to pass a drug screen. And you'll be required to sign a loyalty oath."

Jack had the rare pleasure of seeing Kate Shugak at a complete loss for words. The pleasure was fleeting. She got her jaw back up into working order and inquired in a tone of lethal sweetness, "Am I going to work on the North Slope or am I joining the American Nazi Party?"

Childress flushed a dark red. "It's standard procedure for all prospective employees to sign a loyalty oath."

Kate looked at Jack. "I drove fifty miles on a snow machine and spent eight hours on a train that stopped for moose every two feet so I could pee in a bottle, pledge allegiance to the corporate flag and freeze my ass off on the edge of the Arctic Ocean?"

"Now, Kate," Jack began soothingly.

Kate opened her mouth to melt his ears off.

"A thousand a day," John King said.

"What?" Childress said.

Startled out of her composure for the second time, Kate gaped at King.

"Plus expenses, of course," he added. "Should run you"—he looked at her consideringly—"oh, say, around two-fifty a day?"

"What!" Childress said.

• • •

Jack closed the door behind King and Childress and leaned against it with crossed arms. "Way-ull. Ah giss now you air in thuh erl bidness."

"And Ah cain't even spell it," she replied, but her Southern accent wasn't as good as his. "What really pisses me off is how sure he was I'd say yes."

"Ah, that's just because you've never sold out before."

"Doesn't take long, does it?" she said with a small, rueful smile.

He grinned. "You hungry?" She shook her head, kicked off her Nikes and crossed her stockinged feet on the coffee table. Jack stretched out next to her, sober now. "You mean it when you said you could handle this job?"

She shrugged, and this time he pushed harder. "What would your grandmother say?"

"I don't plan on telling her." She shifted smoothly from

17

defense to offense. "If you were so sure I wouldn't take a job working for an oil company, why did you haul me all the way into town?"

He kissed her. It took a while. When he let her come up for air, she said, "Oh."

He was more than ready to haul her into the bedroom but she wasn't ready to go, and one of Jack Morgan's many talents was an acute ability to read Kate Shugak sign. Still, there was no harm in some friendly persuasion. He slid an arm around her shoulders and pulled her against him. She felt good. He'd missed her. He wondered if she'd missed him, but that way madness lay and he dispatched the thought before it was fully formed. "How's the homestead?"

"Soggy during the day, frozen at night. Breakup SOP."

"Like town." His hand wandered. "Is the creek clear yet?"

Kate shook her head. "It's jammed with ice all the way back up to Twisted Lake."

"Going to flood?"

"I wouldn't be surprised." She grabbed his hand and looked at his watch. "What time is it?"

"Want to know where the leaders are?" Jack used the remote to turn on the television. "I see Mandy and Chick aren't making the run this year."

"Half the team's down with some kind of virus. Look, there. Turn it up."

The cheery twinkie in seed pearls and big hair and shiny earrings the size of manhole covers ran down the Iditarod leaders so quickly it was hard to make sense of the names and cut immediately to another twinkie via satellite reporting local color from Kaltag. This twinkie was enveloped in an oversize parka with the hood pulled so far forward that all that could be seen of his face was a frostbitten nose and a

18

microphone. The picture cut to footage of a barfing dog being loaded onto a Cessna 206 and a few grave words from a gloomy veterinarian, followed by an interview with the Alaskan head of the SPCA, who unburdened himself of an unequivocal and comprehensive denunciation of the sport of dog mushing in general, the race to Nome in particular, all fifty mushers individually and collectively, the Iditarod Trail Committee, the race sponsors and, last but not least, ABC's *Wide World of Sports.*

He paused for breath and Jack turned off the set. "Next stop Shaktoolik, about time for a storm. Who does Mandy say looks good for this year?"

"She says it's DeeDee's turn but that Martin may have other ideas."

Greatly daring, Jack said, "About time for the guys to win a few back-to-back." Kate refused the lure, and he re-baited the hook and cast again. "Besides, the only reason them girl mushers win all the time is because they don't weigh as much as the guys do and they can go faster with fewer dogs."

"Is that so?" Kate said, fascinated with this new insight into the art of dog mushing. "And here I always thought it was because they trained better teams and ran better races."

Jack was betrayed into a laugh.

"Something else I've always wondered," Kate pursued, "why is it that when Rick Swenson mushes into a blizzard to win the Iditarod he's fearless and heroic, but when Libby Riddles does the same thing she's reckless and foolhardy?"

Jack surrendered unconditionally. "Just lucky, I guess." He let his hand slip again. "Did I tell you Michael Armstrong asked me to fly for him this year?"

"Is that right? You could have been a member of the Iditarod Air Force?" He nodded, and she said, "Well? What the hell are you doing sitting here?"

He pointed at the TV screen. "Did that look like fun to you? When they're sick them dogs run from both ends. No, thanks. The Cessna'd never smell the same again." They sat quietly for a few moments. After a bit Kate let her head rest on Jack's shoulder. Encouraged, he said in a low voice, "I know how torn up you were over that damn spill. If you think you can't handle this, I can find someone else."

He couldn't see her face, and she didn't answer at first. Eventually she stirred and said, "We knew the spill was going to happen."

He looked down at the top of her head. "Who's we?"

"The people who live on the Gulf. The Cordova Aquatic Marketing Association, the Cordova District Fishermen United, the Lower Cook Inlet Fishermen's League. Locals. They're fishermen. They know the Narrows. They know the Mother of Storms. They knew it was just a matter of time. They spent a lot of their own money lobbying for the pipeline to go overland through Canada."

Jack kept silent, knowing she wasn't finished.

"I wrote a letter to the governor after the spill, did I tell you?"

"No."

"I told him we ought to kick RPetCo out of the state as an example to other oil companies. Thou Canst Not Shit in Our Nest and Get Away With It. I suggested that with all the lawyers running around Juneau surely to God there had to be some kind of provision in the leases requiring the oil companies to maintain at least minimal environmental standards on pain of revocation of their lease agreements, and that RPetCo had as surely violated that provision, and let us boot them out forthwith."

"You get any answer back?"

"No. So I went down to the offices of the Division of Oil and Gas and looked up the leases, and of course, it's not that simple."

"It never is."

"No. The lessors have to post bonds, but some of the bonds for the smaller contractors are as low as ten grand. The highest one I found was for a million, and that one was for a drill site on the Slope. Some of the leases even say that restoration of the site shall be 'at the discretion of the commissioner.' "

"The commissioner of the Department of Oil and Gas?"

"Yeah."

"Who is a political appointee."

"Yeah."

There was another silence, which Jack broke. "So you would kick RPetCo out of the state if you could."

"Yeah."

"But you can't."

"Nope."

"So you'll work for them instead."

"For a thousand a day."

"Plus expenses."

Kate stretched. "You heard him. Won't be any."

"I guess you'll just have to make up some to justify that two-fifty allowance, then."

"I guess." He felt good against her side, warm and hard. "Besides, given the restricted access and the restricted employee roster, I can't imagine this job is going to take very long. I'll probably be up and back in forty-eight hours."

"You think King really thinks it's a UCo employee?"

"No, and neither does he, or he'd have Childress handling

it. Tell me about the DB."

Jack tucked her head back into his shoulder. "Chuck Cass, thirty-four, production operator, worked for RPetCo since 1980, they brought him up to Prudhoe in 1987 from their Lima plant."

"Lima, Peru?"

"Lima, Ohio."

"Oh. Did he drown?"

"Yeah. But the coroner says he was ready to fly. He was probably on takeoff when he fell into the pool. Childress—"

"He sure is on the prod."

Jack grunted. "Sloper syndrome."

"What's that?"

"Childress makes too much money. He's afraid King's going to take some of it back if you find the dealer before he does." He paused. As security chief Childress was in a perfect position to spot the weak links in the security chain between Slope and town. And Kate was right, he had been on the prod. It might only have been the territorial imperative; it could as easily have been apprehension, even fear.

Kate moved restlessly against him and he said, "Anyway, Childress says a guard found traces of a couple lines of coke on one of the benches in the sauna. They figure he tooted up there and—"

She raised her head. "Wait a minute. A *sauna*?"

Deadpan beneath that incredulous gaze, he said, "Certainly a sauna. It's right off the pool. No well-dressed oil field should be without one."

"A sauna?" she repeated, unable to keep the amazement out of her voice. "A banya, an honest-to-God sweat on the North Slope?"

"Yup."

She considered. "This job might not be so bad after all."

"Can't you think about anything except work?" he complained. "I was hoping to adjourn this encounter to the bedroom and discuss how long it's been since I've seen you. Possibly over a snifter or two of brandy."

She stretched her arms over her head, pulling her shirt tight in interesting places. "Real women drink Diet 7UP." He was just lovesick enough to climb back in the Blazer and slip and slide on up to Carr's for a case of the carbonated beverage of her choice. She was just grateful enough to bestow a suitable reward.

DANA STABENOW
A COLD DAY FOR MURDER

DANA STABENOW
A FATAL THAW

DANA STABENOW
DEAD IN THE WATER

DANA STABENOW
A COLD BLOODED BUSINESS

DANA STABENOW
PLAY WITH FIRE

DANA STABENOW
BLOOD WILL TELL

DANA STABENOW
BREAKUP

DANA STABENOW
KILLING GROUNDS

DANA STABENOW
HUNTER'S MOON

DANA STABENOW
MIDNIGHT COME AGAIN

DANA STABENOW
THE SINGING OF THE DEAD

DANA STABENOW
A FINE AND BITTER SNOW

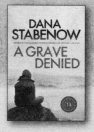

DANA STABENOW
A GRAVE DENIED

DANA STABENOW
A TAINT IN THE BLOOD

DANA STABENOW
A DEEPER SLEEP

DANA STABENOW
WHISPER TO THE BLOOD

DANA STABENOW
A NIGHT TOO DARK

DANA STABENOW
THOUGH NOT DEAD

DANA STABENOW
RESTLESS IN THE GRAVE

DANA STABENOW
BAD BLOOD

Available now

ABOUT
KATE SHUGAK

KATE SHUGAK is a native Aleut working as a private investigator in Alaska. She's 5 foot 1 inch tall, carries a scar that runs from ear to ear across her throat and owns a half-wolf, half-husky dog named Mutt. Resourceful, strong-willed, defiant, Kate is tougher than your average heroine – and she needs to be to survive the worst the Alaskan wilds can throw at her.

To discover more – and some tempting special offers – why not visit our website: www.headofzeus.com

MEET THE AUTHOR

In 1991 Dana Stabenow, born in Alaska and raised on a 75-foot fishing trawler, was offered a three-book deal for the first of her Kate Shugak mysteries. In 1992, the first in the series, *A Cold Day for Murder*, received an Edgar Award from the Crime Writers of America.

You can contact Dana Stabenow via her website: www.stabenow.com